'That was fantastic,' Glenn said laughingly as he took her in his arms and danced her along the main street of the village, past the fairy lights in the windows of the cottages, past the giant Christmas tree in the square where the surgery was, and up the path of the place she called home.

As they faced each other breathlessly at her door Anna wanted to stay in his arms for ever, with everything open and truthful between them. But it was still there—the fear that he would want to marry her out of concern rather than desire if she ever told him what had happened to her.

Sensing that she was retreating behind the wariness that never seemed to go away, he kissed her just once—with a tenderness and passion that made her bones melt.

Taking the door key out of her hand, he unlocked the door of the annexe. As she stepped inside he said, 'Thanks for a wonderful experience,' and went striding off to where Bracken House stood in the darkness of the midnight hour.

**Dear Reader**

Having been brought up happily enough in a Lancashire mill town, where fields and trees were sparse on the landscape, I now live in the countryside and find much pleasure in the privilege of doing so. It gives me the opportunity to write about village life with its caring communities and beautiful surroundings.

So, dear reader, welcome to the first of my four stories about Willowmere, a picturesque village tucked away in the Cheshire countryside. During the changing seasons you will meet the folk who live and work there, and share in their lives and loves.

In this first book, Willowmere is beneath the mantle of winter, and over their first Christmas together in years practice nurse Anna is reunited with her long-lost love Glenn, a handsome doctor. Will the gift of happiness be theirs at this special time? Read on to find out!

*Abigail Gordon*

### The Willowmere Village Stories

*Look out for Georgina and Ben's story in the spring!*

# CHRISTMAS AT WILLOWMERE

BY
ABIGAIL GORDON

MILLS & BOON®
*Pure reading pleasure*™

First published in Great Britain 2008
Harlequin Mills & Boon Limited,
Eton House, 18-24 Paradise Road, Richmond, Surrey TW9 1SR

© Abigail Gordon 2008

ISBN: 978 0 263 19912 3

Set in Times Roman 10½ on 12¾ pt
15-0908-48895

Printed and bound in Great Britain
by Antony Rowe Ltd, Chippenham, Wiltshire

**Abigail Gordon** loves to write about the fascinating combination of medicine and romance from her home in a Cheshire village. She is active in local affairs, and is even called upon to write the script for the annual village pantomime! Her eldest son is a hospital manager, and helps with all her medical research. As part of a close-knit family, she treasures having two of her sons living close by, and the third one not too far away. This also gives her the added pleasure of being able to watch her delightful grandchildren growing up.

**Recent titles by the same author:**

COUNTRY DOCTOR, SPRING BRIDE
A SINGLE DAD AT HEATHERMERE
A WEDDING IN THE VILLAGE
CITY DOCTOR, COUNTRY BRIDE

For Bryan Murray, a fellow writer and my brother

# CHAPTER ONE

THE first snow of winter had fallen during the night and as Anna and the children walked the short distance to the village school it crunched beneath their feet, cold and dazzling beneath a pale sun.

When Pollyanna and Jolyon had awakened to find a white blanket on cottage roofs and gardens there had been cries of delight and breakfast had been a rushed affair, so eager were they to be out of doors and in the snow...and now the three of them were making slow progress. With faces rosy from the cold, the children were stopping every few yards to slide on the slippery surface of the pavement or pausing to scoop up the snow in their woolly mittens.

But at last wellies had been exchanged for trainers, mittens put on a radiator to dry in the school cloakroom, and hats and warm jackets hung on pegs, leaving Anna free to make her way to the village's health care centre where she was a part-time practice nurse.

It was snowing again, swirling flakes resting briefly wherever they fell before turning to wetness. She smiled. It was the beginning of December, early for the first snow of winter to be transforming the village into a wonderland of white.

Not all people saw it as something enchanting. There would be no smiles from those who lived high up on the fringe of the moors, beside the proud peaks that today were snow-capped. Sheep farmers and other remote dwellers would be watching the weather forecasts uneasily and hoping that this was just a fleeting reminder that winter had arrived.

Most of the parents who had dropped their children off at the school had gone. Just a single car was still parked outside, and as she walked past the window on the driver's side it was lowered and a man's voice said questioningly, 'Anna?'

She stopped, hoping that it wasn't a patient wanting a kerbside consultation instead of going to the surgery, and waited as a pair of long legs swung out of the car.

'Glenn!' she breathed, taking a step backwards. 'What are you doing here?'

'I was passing the school and saw you going in with the children,' he said. 'So I stayed around until you came out.'

Anna swallowed hard with legs wobbling beneath her. It was five years since she'd seen the man standing in front of her, and it had felt like an eternity. The last time she'd seen him she'd told him they had no future. That she wasn't going to work in Africa with him because she was needed here in Willowmere. It was where she belonged.

It had been a half-truth. There'd been another reason why she had ended their relationship, a reason that she had not wanted to burden him with as it would have meant him sacrificing a cherished dream on her account.

She'd belonged where *he* was, but life, with its twists

and turns, had shattered all her hopes and dreams on a day such as this, and instead of her future being the happy and fulfilling thing she'd wanted it to be, it had turned onto a narrow restricting path.

After what she'd said to Glenn Hamilton the last time she'd seen him, she'd thought never to see him again. Yet here he was, as large as life, and she couldn't believe it.

They'd met at a disco organised by their respective colleges when she'd been taking a nursing degree and Glenn had been studying to be a doctor. The attraction between them had been instant. They'd spent every spare moment together from that night and as graduation day had drawn near in their last year, they'd begun to make plans for a future they intended to spend together, blissfully confident that nothing was ever going to separate them.

As they faced each other Anna's heartbeat was like a marching army thudding in her breast. On a cold and snowy morning Glenn had appeared in Willowmere again.

He was close enough for her to see that he'd changed since she'd last seen him. He was thinner, his face almost gaunt beneath the dark thatch that lay upon his head, but as their glances held she saw that his eyes, the same deep blue as violets, were the thing about him that had changed most.

There had been enthusiasm and purpose in them once, now there was uncertainty there. The look of someone who wasn't sure of his welcome.

As for the rest of him, he was still tall and straight-backed, and was sporting a tan which looked out of place in the snow of an English winter.

'I just thought I'd look you up,' he said evenly, reminding her of the question she'd gasped out at the sight of him…

'You were *that* sure I would be here after such a long time?' she said quietly.

'I was pretty sure, yes, after you informing me the last time we met that you'd had second thoughts about us and wanted to call it off. That we'd been apart too long, and you needed to help your brother with the children after they lost their mother in an accident.'

Please, don't remind me of that dreadful day, she thought. He would never know what it had cost her to tell him she wanted to finish with him.

'So what has brought you back home?' she asked, without commenting on what he'd just said.

'I'm taking some leave from the job and thought I'd look up my old friends and acquaintances. I left London in the early hours and arrived here just before eight o'clock. Saw what looked like the local hostelry, a place called The Pheasant, and booked in there for a short stay before I did anything else just to be on the safe side, as it's hardly the weather to have to sleep in the car.'

So she'd been delegated to his list of friends and acquaintances, Anna thought, and could she blame him after what she'd done to him? She was drowning in the joy of seeing him in the flesh again instead of in her dreams, but at the same time was hoping she would be able to disguise her delight so that Glenn wouldn't guess that she still cared.

As if reading her thoughts, he said, 'I haven't come

to butt into your life, Anna. I expect you'll have settled down with someone else by now, though the young ones you were with would be your brother's children, I imagine, as they looked the right age.'

'Yes,' she told him steadily, 'Pollyanna and Jolyon started school in September and, no, I'm not with anyone else.' Before he could comment on that she went on quickly, 'I call them Polly and Jolly. They live with their father in the house where he and I grew up next to the surgery. My home is the annexe on the other side of the building. It's a convenient arrangement. I'm near when needed and yet it gives James and I our own space.

'He manages very well under the circumstances, with a busy practice to run and the children to take care of. Obviously they come first in his life and in mine too because they are so young and vulnerable.'

Glenn was staggered to hear her matter-of-fact description of what her life had become, and even more so when he asked about her father and was told, 'Dad died not long ago. He never got over losing my mum. James is in charge of the practice now. I'm employed there from nine o'clock until three now the children are at school, and it is where I should be now. I must ask you to excuse me as we are always busier than usual in this kind of weather.'

'Hop in, then,' he said, turning back to the car. 'I'll take you.'

'It's only a short distance. I'll be there in minutes,' she protested.

'Nevertheless, I'll take you. For one thing, it's bad underfoot and you'll be no use to anyone if you fall and hurt yourself.'

'All right,' she agreed, and slid into the passenger seat, so aware of his nearness she had to look away. She felt her manner had been too abrupt and as she pointed the way to the surgery said, 'I'm sorry I'm in such a rush. I wish you'd let me know you were coming.'

He raised a quizzical eyebrow. 'Would you really have wanted me to?'

She didn't answer. Anna was content with her life up to a point as long as she didn't dwell on the fact that she wasn't going anywhere fast, because if she did it made her think wistfully of the full and exciting life that Glenn must be leading in Africa, yet when she looked at Pollyanna and Jolyon secure in happy childhood, there was comfort to be had.

But now she'd just discovered that Glenn wasn't in Africa. He was here in Willowmere, near enough to touch, and it felt unreal.

As she was debating whether to invite him to call when he was passing to make up for her lack of cordiality, he forestalled her by saying, 'Would you feel like joining me for a drink at The Pheasant this evening? It would be nice to have a chat. I've been wondering how things were with you.'

'Er…yes…I suppose I could,' she said slowly, 'and everything is fine.'

It wasn't, of course. The secret she'd kept from him would make sure of that, but Glenn was never going to know about the thing that lay so heavily upon her heart…

'On weekdays the four of us have our evening meal together at Bracken House,' she explained. 'It will be eightish before I've cleared away and done a few chores.'

'Whatever time suits you will suit me,' he said easily.

This polite chit-chat was weird, Anna was thinking as he stopped the car in front of the surgery. Did Glenn remember how they used to be when they were at university?

When his lectures were over he would cross London to where she was based and come knocking on her study door. Once inside he would coax her away from her books and they'd go to a café or the students' union and would be so engrossed in each other they wouldn't notice what they were eating.

He had been the idealist, eager to use his medical knowledge to put the world to rights. Unlike her, he hadn't had any family to consider. He'd been an only child. His parents had divorced when he'd been quite young and he'd spent his childhood being passed from one to the other. He'd lost touch with them once he'd turned eighteen and had become quite self-sufficient as a result.

They'd planned that if they got the degrees they wanted they would go to Africa to join one of the aid programmes. At some time in the future they would get married, either out there or back home, and then have children, something that Glenn saw as very important, having had no proper family life of his own.

That had been before her mother had died unexpectedly from a major heart attack, leaving her father, who had been senior partner at the surgery for many years, frail and inconsolable.

At the same time her sister-in-law, Julie, who had been expecting twins, had been having a difficult pregnancy with dangerously high blood pressure. She had been in hospital, confined to bed, and monitored all the time to check for signs of pre-eclampsia and Anna had known that she couldn't leave the country with all that happening.

Unlike Glenn's childhood, hers had been magical. She'd been surrounded by love and whenever she'd mentioned it he'd said, 'That is how it's going to be for our children. They won't have to listen to endless rows and feel lost and bewildered all the time like I did when I was a kid.'

She'd nodded her agreement, happy and secure in their love for each other and having no idea that the fates had some ideas of their own regarding that, and now she felt like pinching herself to see if she was awake. She was meeting Glenn at The Pheasant in a few hours' time, something that she would have thought as likely as the sun falling out of the sky.

'You may not find the pub very exciting,' she warned as she opened the car door. 'It's usually village affairs being discussed on a winter night. On a summer evening it's a different matter. The place is full of walkers and tourists and the regulars don't get a look-in.'

'Whatever it is like, I shall enjoy it,' he told her, ready to depart. 'I'll say goodbye until this evening, then.'

As Glenn drove towards The Pheasant to unload his belongings he was wondering if that was the worst over.

He'd spent five years in various African countries, doing what he'd set out to do, and now he was ready for a spell of normal life back home, and every time he thought of normal life he thought of Anna.

There had been no one for him since she'd told him

their relationship was over. He hadn't had the time or the inclination, though he knew deep down that he needed to move on. But before he did so he'd felt he had to see Anna one more time to make sure that there was nothing left of what they'd once had.

So now here he was in the Cheshire village that was so dear to her heart, grateful that he'd found her still there. If what she'd said was correct, just as he had never replaced her, so she had never put anyone in his place, though that didn't have to mean anything. But it had been an uneasy moment when he'd seen her walking along in the snow with a couple of kids. His spirits had sunk to the soles of his feet but common sense had reminded him that her brother's children would be that age.

As he'd driven up from London he'd wondered, as he had many times before, how she would greet him if he found her still there. The memory of their last meeting was still cuttingly clear, and now he had his answer. There'd been no happy reunion. Just the exchange of a few stilted sentences had told him he'd been a fool to expect anything else after the way she'd dumped him all that time ago.

When they'd got their degrees he'd ended up going to Africa without her. It had been at Anna's suggestion because her life had been taken over by family commitments, as she'd always thought it might be.

'As soon as Dad is on the mend and Julie has had the babies, I'll join you,' she'd promised, and he'd reluctantly agreed to leave her behind.

They'd kept in contact all the time and on each occasion when they'd spoken Anna had told him how much she was missing him and longing to be there beside him. When she'd phoned to say that the babies had arrived safely and her father was no worse, he'd hoped that soon they would be together.

At that time, along with other members of his team, he'd been about to do a month-long trip to remote areas where the people rarely had the chance to receive health care, and he'd hoped that by the time he returned Anna would be ready with the date of her arrival.

But there had been no messages waiting for him when he got back and every time he'd rung her there was no answer. He'd felt a sense of foreboding and after two weeks of no contact he'd taken leave and flown home, going straight to Willowmere with all speed.

When Anna had opened the door of Bracken House to him he'd thought she looked ghastly and his anxiety had increased. As she'd stepped back to let him in he'd asked, 'What's wrong, Anna? Why haven't you answered my calls?'

'I've been too busy,' she said, and he observed her in disbelief.

'Too busy to let me know when you're coming to join me? We've already been apart too long. I've been living for the day.'

'Glenn, look, I'm sorry but I'm not coming,' had been the next stab to the heart. 'Julie and I were in an accident. Mercifully the babies were unharmed and I was…hurt but survived. But Julie…she was killed. So I can't leave the little ones now.' She sighed and put up a hand to stop him saying anything. 'I'm sorry to do this to you, but even before it happened I'd been giving a lot of thought to us. I was going to call it off, yet didn't want to do it over the phone, but now that you're here, I can at least tell you to your face.'

'What?' He stared at her aghast. She said it like a well-rehearsed speech. 'The last time we spoke you said you would be joining me soon. I understand why you can't go to Africa, but we can change our plans. I can come back to work in Britain. We can live here where your family are, so that they have you near, but it doesn't have to affect our relationship surely. What has made you have doubts about us?'

Anna shook her head. 'It's no good, Glenn. I've fallen out of love with you. I've had time to step back and take a look at where I was heading and have changed my mind.'

'Are you telling me in a roundabout way that there's someone else?' he asked harshly.

'No. I'm just telling you that I want out. I've changed my mind.'

'Because Julie has died?'

'Partly, but not just because of that.'

'So what else, then?'

'I've told you, I've just had time to think about things. About us. It's not going to work. Will you please go?'

'Yes. I will,' he said coldly, and followed it with, 'I'm so sorry about what has happened. Give your brother my condolences. I'll see myself out.'

He went back to Africa the day after she'd demoralised him with her change of heart, and there had been no communication of any kind from her since the day she'd dumped him without the slightest warning. He'd thrown himself into his difficult and often dangerous work in an attempt to forget her and forced himself to move on.

So why had he come back now? Gazing through the mullioned window of a pleasant chintzy bedroom beneath the eaves of The Pheasant later that morning, he knew it was need that had brought him here.

For a long time he'd been bound by the needs of others. Now it was his own need that was driving him. He was drained mentally and physically after what he'd had to do and what he'd had to observe, and ached for Anna's presence in his life once more, but when he recalled the way she had wiped out what they'd had together in just a few abrupt sentences he hadn't any high hopes regarding that.

He'd been lost for words when she'd told him of the passing of her father. What kind of a life had she been living during the years they'd been apart? he wondered. He could have helped make it easier if she'd given him the chance.

Maybe the coming evening would bring a better understanding between them, but he wasn't too hopeful. Getting to know Anna again was not going to be easy.

Physically she hadn't changed as much as he had. The red-gold of her hair was the same, although instead of hanging long on her shoulders, as it used to, it was now in a short, smooth bob framing a face that had no special claim to beauty other than big hazel eyes with long lashes and a kind mouth.

Personality-wise it seemed a different thing, and he supposed he shouldn't be surprised. Trying to fill the gap that their mother had left for those two children and being there for her father and brother must have left little time for her to pursue her own life.

He had never experienced family closeness such as hers. His home life had been a poor thing by comparison and it was why he longed for children of his own, so that he could give them the love that he'd never had.

After years of mayhem in war-torn lands, it had felt as if this beautiful village, which had always meant so much to Anna, had been beckoning him, and he'd decided to have one last sighting of her before he closed the pages of a book that was only half-written.

So far he'd accomplished two things. He'd found her out there on the snow-covered street and she'd agreed to meet up with him later. With regard to anything else, he was prepared to wait and see.

James was in Reception, talking to Elaine Ferguson, the practice manager, when Anna came through the main doors of the surgery, and he saw immediately that something was amiss.

When he'd finished speaking to Elaine he followed her into the smaller of the two rooms where the nurses performed their functions and asked, 'What's wrong? You look like you're in shock. You didn't have problems getting the children to school, did you?'

She managed a smile. 'I encountered some reluctance to leave the snow behind, but once they were inside and settled they were fine.'

'So what is it, then?'

'I've just met someone I haven't seen in years.'

'Who?'

'Glenn Hamilton.'

'The guy you met at university?'

'Yes. He's back home for a while and looking up old friends.'

'So what's wrong with that?'

'Nothing, I suppose. It was just a shock, seeing him here in Willowmere,' she said, thinking how that was putting it mildly!

At the time she'd broken up with Glenn the only things that had been registering with James had been his wife's death, the needs of his children and his sister's recovery from her injuries. What had been going on in her private life had been a blur, and in any case he'd never met Anna's boyfriend.

'So where has he been all this time?'

'He's a doctor and has been working with one of the aid organisations in Africa. 'It's what I've always wanted to do but the accident put paid to that.'

'I've never heard you say that before!' he exclaimed.

'Why would I mention it?' she said gently. 'It belongs to the past. Though it is something I might do in years to come.' And the thought was there that it wouldn't be the same without Glenn beside her.

'And he wants to see you again for old times' sake, is that it?'

She shrugged. 'So it appears. Glenn has booked into The Pheasant for a few days and because I didn't have time when we met to talk to him properly, I've agreed to meet him there tonight for a drink. You haven't got anything planned, have you?'

'No,' he said immediately, 'and if I had I would cancel it. Why don't you ask him round for a meal? I'd like to meet him. Any friend of yours is a friend of mine, though I don't recall you ever mentioning him much in the past.'

'There was nothing to tell. He went working abroad and we kept in touch for a while and that was it. The Glenn I knew in those days was clever and caring in his approach to medicine. That was why he was so eager to help the world's suffering.'

'You weren't in love with him then?'

Her reply was evasive. 'We were close at one time but it didn't work out.' She glanced around her. 'And I'm here to work, aren't I? Though surprisingly there doesn't seem to be anyone needing to see a nurse at this moment.'

'There soon will be,' James promised, and putting to one side for the moment the discussion they'd just had he went to call in his next patient.

But as the morning progressed and those who had come to consult him came and went, it kept coming back, and he thought, as he'd done a thousand times, that he owed his children's wellbeing and his sanity to his sister.

It had been she who had been there for him during days and months of despair after he'd lost Julie, and at the same time she'd helped look after the babies that had been left without a mother, while making a slow recovery from her own injuries.

It concerned him constantly that she'd had to put her plans on hold for their father's sake and his, yet every time he brought up the subject Anna always told him gently that she was fine and he would be the first to know when she wasn't.

He'd been able to tell from what she'd said that the

Hamilton fellow had been a close friend. He remembered Anna saying that someone from university had called some weeks after the accident, but he'd been at the practice at the time and with so much on his mind it had barely registered.

During Anna's last year at university and when she'd come home at the end of it, he'd been so concerned over Julie's difficult pregnancy and his father's failing health that what had been going on in his sister's life had passed him by.

For instance, he hadn't known until today that she'd wanted to work abroad when she'd qualified and had given up that idea because she'd been needed back home. They'd always been a close and loving family but Anna's devotion had gone way beyond the call of duty.

He supposed he should have married again, giving her back the freedom she'd so willingly forfeited. But the thought of replacing Julie was more than he could bear, and if he ever did meet someone who came near to her in his affections, would she want a widower with two young children for a husband? Anna adored Polly and Jolly just as much as he did, but his was the responsibility.

There had been blood tests to do during the morning, along with injections, dressings to change and other duties that went with the job for Anna and Beth Jackson, the other practice nurse, and as always the time flew past. There was no opportunity to think about the evening ahead but when three o'clock came and it was time to pick up the children, seeing Glenn again was the thought uppermost in her mind...

He is here in Willowmere, she thought incredulously as she waited for them to come out of school. I can see The Pheasant from my bedroom window just five minutes' walk away and I may as well enjoy the thought while it lasts, as nothing will have changed by the time he is ready to leave. I just can't blight his life. He deserves better than I can give him.

When they arrived home Pollyanna and Jolyon played in the garden in the snow until the light faded and then she brought them in for a change of clothes and a warm drink, and all the time she was wishing that the hands of the clock would move faster.

She dressed with care for the evening ahead in the colours that suited her best. Dark green trousers and a short cream jacket with a long scarf to match showed off the red-gold of her hair and the beautiful hazel eyes that once had been clear and cloudless.

She'd changed a lot over recent years but tonight she wanted Glenn to see that she was still the same woman as before. There was no need for him to ever know what she'd given up for him, or feel sorry for the life she was leading now.

It had been an act of love and if she sometimes felt she should have given him a choice, she put the thought firmly from her mind. He was the idealist and might have said it didn't matter, which would have left her in a limbo state of always wondering if he regretted his decision. No, she had done the right thing.

Anyway, he was here now, and maybe he didn't hate her as much as she'd thought he would. He'd seemed friendly enough towards her, and she'd even sensed compassion in him when she'd told him about her father, but whatever his life was like now, she knew there would still be bitterness in him for the way she'd treated him, and she couldn't blame him.

But, she decided firmly, he had come to Willowmere of his own accord, so why not make the most of it for the short time he was there? Picking up her bag and keys she went out into the snowy night.

# CHAPTER TWO

THE accident had happened just as Anna had been ready to let Glenn know she was flying out to join him. The babies were a month old and it had seemed as if she might be no longer needed at Bracken House with Julie back to her normal self, the problem of the high blood pressure having disappeared once she'd given birth. And with James around to keep an eye on their father, the time had seemed right.

Glenn had still been out of contact but was due back soon on the day that she'd driven Julie and the children to the hospital to have their feet checked by a paediatric consultant while James had held the fort at the surgery.

Both babies had been born with feet slightly inward turning, due to being in a cramped position in the womb, and had immediately been put into tiny boots that would correct the problem. And on an icy winter morning she and Julie had taken them for a progress check.

The report had been good. They'd told the anxious mother that it was a common enough thing and as it was being treated promptly it should soon right itself.

They'd set off for home in good spirits and all had been fine until a car coming fast out of a minor road had skidded into them on the icy surface and hit the side where Julie had been sitting.

By some miracle, the babies hadn't been hurt, but their mother had taken the full impact of a car much heavier car than theirs and by the time the emergency services had arrived she had died from severe head and spinal injuries.

Anna had been found injured in the driver's seat, not too seriously at first glance, but in great pain in the pelvic area.

As a paramedic had bent over her she'd heard the babies crying and gasped through the pain and shock, 'The babies!'

'They seem all right,' the paramedic told her. 'They're being lifted out of the car now.'

'And their mother?'

'We're doing all we can,' he said gently. 'And now, before we move you, tell me where the pain is.'

'Everywhere,' she moaned weakly, 'but worse around my pelvis.' She'd drifted off into nothingness for a few moments and the next thing she knew she was being lifted carefully onto a stretcher before being put into an ambulance.

She knew she'd lost Julie as soon as she saw James's face in A and E. On the point of being taken to X-Ray she'd told him to go back to the babies, that she would be all right, though she wasn't as confident as she sounded.

Her life changed for ever when a gynaecologist stood by her bedside and said apologetically, 'I'm afraid that the news isn't good, Anna.'

She'd had severe bruising of the chest and broken ribs, but the most attention was being given to the injuries to her pelvis and uterus, and his next words explained why.

'I'm going to have to do a hysterectomy. Your uterus is too badly damaged for me not to do so.'

'Oh, no!' she groaned. 'Not that. We wanted children!' And as the tears had slid down her cheeks she could hear Glenn's voice in her mind saying, *Our children will be born into a loving family, Anna.* What would he say when he knew there wasn't going to be any?

She cried and cried for what she and Glenn would never have and longed for him to be there to comfort her, but he was far away out of reach somewhere in Africa, and by the time he was due back she'd made her decision.

Glenn wasn't going to be put in the position of having to choose between her and a life with children, she'd decided. He would be spared that because she wasn't going to tell him about the surgery she'd had to undergo. She loved him too much for that. When next they spoke she was going to finish it.

When Anna appeared in the doorway of The Pheasant Glenn got to his feet immediately and came towards her, smiling his welcome, and she wondered if he'd forgiven her for what she'd done and the cold, abrupt manner with which she'd done it.

It had been the only way she could make the break at the time because she'd been hurting so much. Losing Julie and knowing that the tender trap with James and the babies was opening up before her had been painful enough, but most of all she'd been hurting because when it came to children of her own, there wouldn't be any.

She'd often questioned if she'd been fair in not telling him what had happened to her. Glenn had been denied the opportunity to make his own decision, but it was all in the past and she'd done what she'd thought right at the time. Whatever the reason for his return, at least they could be friends, and she returned his smile with a beam of her own that made his eyes widen.

'So tell me about it,' she said when they were seated with drinks in front of them beside a glowing log fire.

'What?'

'Africa, of course.'

'It was a fulfilling experience and one day I will go back,' he said quietly, 'but not yet. It was also dangerous, demoralising and exhausting, but I never had any regrets, except maybe one.'

Anna didn't ask what that was. She had a feeling that she knew, but it seemed that he was going to tell her anyway. 'You weren't with me.'

'I would have been no use to you if I had been,' she retorted quickly. 'My mind would have been back here all the time, with James struggling with the children without Julie and myself, his family all dead or absent.'

Glenn wasn't smiling now, his jaw taut. 'If you remember, I told you at the time we could have got round it. You wouldn't have called it off for just that. There had to be another reason.'

'I don't want us to spend our time harking back to the past while you're here,' she said, shying away from the moment. 'Can't we be like you said, old friends renewing their acquaintance after a long time? Though I'm surprised that you haven't found someone else by now.'

'Why? Have you?'

'Er…no.'

He shrugged. 'So there you are.' He decided a change of subject was called for. Anna had been lit up a moment ago and he wanted her to stay that way, though he didn't flatter himself it was anything to do with him, unless she was out to show him that she wasn't the Cinderella figure he might be seeing her as.

After that they chatted generally. Glenn asked in detail about the surgery, said he'd never had any experience of a country practice, so she suggested he pop in and she would give him the guided tour. The evening moved along pleasantly enough until the landlord announced time.

'I'll walk you home,' he said.

She shook her head. 'No need. I can see my place from here.' And because she was anxious to know, she asked, 'How long are you intending staying in Willowmere?'

'Just a few days. Why?'

'Would you like to have dinner with us tomorrow?'

She saw his face stretch and thought surely he didn't think she wouldn't offer him some hospitality.

'I'd love to, if you are sure,' he replied. 'I'd like to meet your brother and Pollyanna and Jolyon.'

'Shall we say six o'clock? I always prepare the evening meal for the four of us and James comes up as soon as the late surgery is over. The children go to bed at half past seven, which gives time for their meal to settle.'

'Six o'clock it is,' he said trying to conceal the pleasure it was giving him in saying it.

* * *

There was a light on at Bracken House when she got back and she stopped off before going to her own place. She found James still up and told him, 'I've done as you said and invited Glenn to eat with us tomorrow night.'

'Good,' he said, looking up from the paperwork in front of him. 'I look forward to meeting him.'

Now that she'd extended the invitation, Anna wasn't sure that she'd done the right thing. Was it a good idea to get so chummy when he would be leaving so soon? Yet why not make the most of every moment? The time they spent together would be something to hold onto when he'd gone.

The next morning at the surgery Beth said, 'The bush telegraph has been buzzing. Who was the handsome guy you were with in The Pheasant last night?'

Anna smiled. It was a fact that not much went unnoticed in Willowmere. It was a close-knit community. Some of the people had lived there all their lives, as their fathers had before them.

'It was just a friend from my university days,' she explained as they called in the first of those waiting to be seen.

Sam Gibson had been passed on to them to have blood taken to assess sugar levels by Georgina Adams, the other full-time doctor in the practice, and he was not happy when he saw the needle.

'It won't take a second, Sam,' Anna told him. 'Look the other way.'

He was a farmer from the outskirts of the village, a big burly fellow afraid of nothing except the needle, so it seemed.

'Don't tell my Dorothy that I was scared of the needle, will you?' he said sheepishly as he rolled his sleeve back down. 'I kid her about being afraid of spiders, so she'll never let it drop if she finds out.'

Smiling, she showed him out then ushered in her next patient, a young girl with a urine infection who James wanted a sample from. And so the morning progressed, though Anna was still gripped by the feeling of unreality that had been there ever since she'd seen Glenn outside the school.

In a spare moment between patients she wondered wryly what people would think if they knew that she'd once been going to marry the man she'd been seen with in The Pheasant. That she'd been crazy not to?

As Anna prepared the meal that evening she was acutely aware that Glenn was going to be seated across the table from her, with James and the children looking on curiously at the stranger in their midst.

She was tempted to get out the best china and then decided not to as she didn't want him to read anything into the invitation that wasn't there. It was a Wednesday and they always had chicken casserole for first course and sticky toffee pudding for dessert, and knowing that the children would be disappointed if those things weren't on offer, she stayed with the usual menu and hoped that it would appeal to their guest.

When they'd met outside the school yesterday Glenn had been wearing a thick jacket over a black sweater and jeans, and she surmised that he might be feeling the cold after being in warmer climates for so long.

But when he rang the doorbell at six o'clock and she opened the door to him with the children, one on either side of her, Anna saw that he'd changed into lighter clothing in the form of a smart suit with shirt and tie.

At once she wished that she *had* got out the best china, that her face wasn't flushed from the heat of the oven, and that she'd found time to dress in something that didn't detract from her appearance of the night before. Yet did it matter? Glenn was going to be just a ship that passed in the night. It was amazing that he'd actually taken the trouble to seek her out.

'Hello again,' he said, and with a smile for the children as she stepped back to let him in, he added, 'I hope I'm not too early.'

'No, of course not,' she told him. 'James isn't here yet, so can I offer you a drink before we eat?''

He wasn't looking so drawn, she thought as she showed him into the sitting room. Maybe he'd spent the day relaxing. She wasn't to know that his less drawn expression was due more to the relief of having crossed the first hurdle in getting to know her again.

While the children played with their toys and the two adults drank a pre-dinner sherry, Glenn said, with his gaze on Pollyanna and Jolyon, 'We've both moved on since we last saw each other, haven't we, Anna?'

'I would describe my life more as moving sideways rather than on,' she commented whimsically. To avoid getting into deep water again, she went on, 'What are you going to do if you don't go back to Africa straight away?'

'I haven't made up my mind yet,' he told her, and was

prevented from saying more by the appearance of James.

When they'd been introduced Anna left the two men chatting while she went into the kitchen to serve the meal. The children followed and, remembering how she'd told them that the visitor was a friend of hers from when she was learning to be a nurse, Polly, who was usually the spokeswoman for the two of them, asked, 'Is that why Dr. Hamilton has come to see us?'

'Yes. He's visiting people he used to know and I was one of them.' Remembering their brief reunion outside the school the day before, when he hadn't shown any reaction to her comment about the way they'd parted, she was wondering why he'd included her on his list.

'Has he been where there are crocodiles?' Jolyon wanted to know.

He was the quieter of the two, and a solemn child, considering her pet name for him, but he usually came up with something imaginative when he made the effort.

'I don't know,' she replied. 'Why don't you ask him?'

'Yes. I will,' he promised.

'You have two captivating children,' Glenn told James as they seated themselves around the table. Jolyon had just asked his question and his eyes had widened as Glenn had explained that there had been crocodiles in some of the places where he'd worked, but as they spent a lot of time in the water he hadn't seen much of them.

'We think so, don't we, Anna?' James said with an affectionate glance at his sister. 'When my wife died, leaving me with two young babies, Anna was a huge help, but it concerns me that she gets so little time to herself. And I'm sure that other people who know her feel the same.'

'Don't do this to me, James,' Anna was begging silently. Don't describe me as someone to be sorry for. Not in front of Glenn. He will soon be going back to where he came from and that is how it has to be.

Silence had fallen over the room and after a moment she said, 'How many times do I have to tell you that I don't mind, James? The children are everything to me.'

And if that isn't telling me straight to go back to where I've come from, I don't know what is, Glenn thought grimly.

But James had been observing Anna and Glenn. He sensed an awareness of each other that they were trying to conceal, and he asked casually, 'So what are you planning to do in the near future, Glenn? Have a rest until you go back? Or look for a position over here for a while?'

'I want to work in the UK for a change,' he told him, 'to recharge my batteries. I've no immediate plans to go back at the moment. I wouldn't mind some general practice work. The sort of thing you do. I have been working in surgeries of a kind for the last few years. They were ill-equipped places, but surgeries nevertheless.'

James nodded but made no comment, and once the meal was over and the children were yawning he said, 'If you'll excuse me, I'll take the children up to bed and leave you and Anna to continue getting reacquainted.'

Pollyanna and Jolyon said goodnight and silence returned once they'd gone, hanging over Anna and Glen like a cloud of uncertainty until he said, 'James seems concerned about you.'

'Yes, I know, but he doesn't need to be. I'm fine,' she

said breezily. 'I'd rather we talked about you than me.
You must have lots to tell about what you've been
doing.'

He wanted to talk about them, not Africa, and said,
'Some other time maybe?'

'What other time?' she questioned. 'You'll be leaving soon.'

'That is, or was, my intention,' he said, and she
wondered what that was supposed to mean. The answer
was in what he said next. 'It is a joy to come to somewhere like this, where it's cold, crisp and clean.'

'You mean to say that you're thinking of extending
your visit?' she asked, not sure where this was leading.
'The snow will be gone in a couple of days, you know,
it's very early. January to March is when we get the
really heavy falls, and how will you occupy yourself in
the countryside in wintertime?'

She couldn't believe she was trying to dissuade him
from staying longer when she hadn't seen him in years.
But she had something to hide and the longer Glenn was
around the more likely it was that he might find out.
Although the only people who knew about it were
James and herself, and he would never discuss her
private affairs with anyone.

'Are you by any chance hinting that you would like
to see me gone?' he asked dryly, and she felt the colour
rise in her cheeks.

'No, of course not,' she told him hurriedly. 'You
must do what is best for yourself.'

Was she out of her mind, she thought, trying to
persuade him to leave when he was inclined to linger? She
might never see him again after this, but nothing had

changed, had it? If he'd come back hoping she might have changed her mind about their relationship, she still couldn't give him a child and nothing was going to alter that.

Yet she had found a degree of contentment in her life and needed to hang onto it. Would she be able to do that with Glenn in Willowmere?

At that moment James appeared to say that the children were asleep and would Glenn like to see the surgery? He was on his feet in an instant, commenting that he would be most interested to see how a country practice functioned.

'It functions very well,' she told him coolly. 'You will be amazed.'

When they came back Glenn was smiling. 'Very impressive,' he said with a gleam in his eye that told her he'd got the message. 'Especially the computer centre in the basement, where the practice manager keeps her finger on the pulse. And now, if you will excuse me, I'll head off back to The Pheasant. I know you both lead very busy lives, and I don't think entertaining would normally be on the agenda on a weekday evening, so I'll say goodnight.' He turned to James and shook his hand. 'It's been a pleasure to meet you and your children, James.'

It was the same as the night before. Anna didn't want them to have to separate and on the spur of the moment she said, 'James has given you the guided tour of the surgery that I promised, but if you like I'll show you some of the village beneath a full moon. Willowmere covered in snow in the moonlight is something to see.'

'I'd like that,' he said, taken aback, and when she'd grabbed a coat and put boots on they went outside. 'Are you trying to confuse me, Anna?' he asked as they walked down the path. 'One moment you are hastening me on my way and the next you are dangling your beautiful village in front of me like a carrot, and considering that it's called Willowmere, I can't see any willow trees at a glance.'

'You won't,' she told him. 'Not here anyway, but on the edge of the village at the foot of the peaks there is a lake and they are there in profusion. From Willow Lake came Willowmere many years ago when people began to move into the area around it, and once you've seen the lake you will know why they came. The trees may be short of a few leaves at this time of year, but they're never bare, and it's a beautiful place no matter what the season.'

'Hmm, it sounds like it. Why don't you and the children show it to me tomorrow after school is over? If it isn't too far, we might get there before the light goes and then we could go for afternoon tea somewhere. I'll call for you.'

'Oh…yes, all right,' she agreed, taken unawares by the suggestion, yet it did have its appeal. It would give her the opportunity to show Glenn some of the reasons why she loved this place and Willow Lake was high on the list. Though she would rather have taken him there on a spring day, or in summer when the weeping willows hung over the water in an abundance of fresh greenery.

But Glenn wouldn't be around then and she didn't want to think about that, even though his arrival was like having a wound that had healed open up again.

As they strolled along the main street with its quaint shops and onto the bridge that spanned the river he asked, 'Are there any eating places around here that would be open and suitable to take the children to at this time of the year?'

She nodded. 'Yes. There's the very place, over there. The Hollyhocks Tea Rooms, a couple of doors away from the post office. They're open all year round and the food is always good. The owners of the place are friends of mine.'

'So the Hollyhocks Tea Rooms it shall be,' he said, 'where Cheshire cheese and Lancashire hotpot will, no doubt, be on the menu as we aren't far from where the two counties meet.'

'And what's wrong with that?' she asked, sending him a look as the moon scudded behind a cloud and they were left in cold, velvet darkness.

'I didn't say there was anything wrong,' he replied hastily, hiding a smile. Then he saw the teasing sparkle in her eyes.

'You know we still have the stocks in the village for those who misbehave,' she joked, 'and we pelt them with rotten eggs. So beware!'

'What?' he exclaimed in assumed horror. 'I would have thought a place as perfect as this would only be able to *lay* its hands on fresh free-range chuckies.'

As they laughed together it was like the old days for a moment. They'd been happy and carefree when they'd first met. In a moment of weakness Anna wished they could go back to those early days.

'What are you thinking?' he asked, observing the change in her expression.

'Nothing,' she said flatly. 'I was just remembering, that's all.'

'So you've not forgotten how it used to be?'

'No. Of course I haven't! Have you?'

'No. I haven't forgotten either,' he told her, and could have gone on to remind her that during their last year at university all his hopes and dreams had been formed and she had demolished them with just a few words. But what was the point? It had all been long ago…

'We've both missed out on many things since then,' he said gravely, 'and I still don't know why.'

At that moment the moon appeared again and he saw her expression in its light. 'What?' he asked. 'What's wrong, Anna?'

'Nothing,' she said quickly. Desperate to lighten the moment, she pointed to an ancient stone building beside the river. 'That's an old water mill. It isn't used now, of course, but it's a favourite with local artists.'

'I can imagine it would be,' he said absently, still concerned about how she'd looked a moment ago. But it was clear that she wasn't going to tell him what was wrong so he said easily, 'I seem to have seen quite a few things tonight, but one thing you haven't shown me is where you live. When do I get to see that? I'd like to be able to picture you there when I've gone.'

'Another time maybe,'' she promised. 'I'll show you round some time, but I think maybe we should call it a day now.'

She was feeling too emotional to take him into her smart little dwelling. Outside in the cold it wasn't hard to keep at a distance but in a more confined space she couldn't guarantee anything.

* * *

When she arrived home James was on the point of putting the ironing board away and on the kitchen table was a neat pile of newly ironed laundry.

'You didn't have to do that,' she protested.

'I know,' he replied. 'Just the same as you don't have to look after me and mine, but you do.' He observed her keenly. 'I liked Glenn. It takes some guts to do what he's been doing.'

'Yes, it does,' she agreed, and wondered what was coming next.

'How would you feel if I offered him a temporary locum position in the practice until he's decided what he wants to do permanently?' he asked, choosing his words carefully. 'I feel he could be just what we need if he agrees. I will have to consult Georgina, of course, though I can't see her objecting to more help around the place. It's what *you* think of the idea that I'm most concerned about. Would you want him living in the village, working in the practice, back in your life to some degree?'

Anna was gazing at him open-mouthed. 'I know you've been thinking of employing a locum for some time,' she croaked, 'but Glenn! You hardly know him.'

'That may be true,' James pointed out equably, 'but *you* know him so it will depend on what you say whether I offer him the position.'

She took a deep breath. Was this the moment to tell James just how close she and Glenn had once been? That he had once been the love of her life, but because she couldn't give him children she had sent him away?

Or was it the time to burden herself with another secret, this time kept from James, and let him go on thinking she and Glenn were just casual friends?

Otherwise he would be devastated to know just how much the operation had ruined her life and it might show through when he was in Glenn's company. It didn't seem as if there was much of a choice.

She took a deep breath. 'You are putting me on the spot, asking me to give my opinion. Glenn and I were close once but we drifted apart, like students do, and as you know I haven't seen him in a long time. But I can tell you one thing with regard to how good a doctor he will be. I have a very clear picture of that. I'm confident that you would find him extremely capable and caring. He would be an asset to the practice. Glenn sailed through every exam and was top of his year at university.

'We would be fortunate to have him on board and I would say go for it if that is what you want. But don't expect anything to change as far as I'm concerned. My life is mapped out and I don't anticipate taking any side turnings. Just so you know, he's offered to take the children and me to the Hollyhocks Tea Rooms tomorrow afternoon after I've shown him the lake. But before you get any crazy ideas, we've no plans to socialise after that.'

'And if I offer him the job?'

'It will be between the two of you. Just make sure he realises that I had nothing to do with it, and give some thought to where he is going to stay if he accepts.'

'Well, the spare bedroom here has an en suite, as you know, so I can accommodate him temporarily if he accepts my offer. I don't think having the kids around would bother him. It's easy to see he's good with children, and you are only next door.'

'I can see that your mind is made up,' she said, still bemused by this latest turn of events.

'Only if you are in favour of the arrangement, and don't forget he has yet to be asked.'

'Yes, I know, and if he agrees it probably won't be for long. He'll soon be off on his travels again. So, yes, it's all right by me, and now I'm going home or I'll never be up on time in the morning.'

'Promise me you won't stay awake, worrying,' he begged, 'as nothing may come of it.'

'I'll do my best,' she said, and went to have a peep at Polly and Jolly before going to the annexe next door. As she looked down at them, beautiful and innocent in sleep, Anna felt peace descend on her.

She might have just done the wrong thing, but wasn't it better to keep up the charade of Glenn being just an acquaintance rather than never to see him again? That was what would have happened if she'd told James not to offer him the position.

# CHAPTER THREE

SLEEP evaded her, as she'd known it would after the events of the day. She heard the church clock strike one, and was still wide awake.

James had been right to consider asking Glenn to join the practice, she thought. What had been between them was long gone, even though he had appeared out of the blue and taken her breath away.

Unlike herself, Glenn had no family to share his life with. It was possible he might appreciate the chance to sample living in the countryside. He'd been prepared to do that when Julie had died and must still wonder why she'd rejected the suggestion and ended their relationship, especially as he'd discovered on his return that there was no one else in her life.

She'd agreed to James's suggestion for both their sakes, and Glenn would have nothing to lose if he accepted, but for the sake of keeping him near she was making a difficult situation even more complicated.

Yet why worry about something that might never happen? she told herself. The odds were that the thought of actually living in Willowmere, as compared to a short visit, would make Glenn refuse James's offer.

\* \* \*

Anna hadn't been the only one finding sleep hard to come by. In his room at The Pheasant, Glenn was reliving every moment from his first sight of her on the snow-covered pavement, taking the children to school.

He'd remembered where she lived, had been to Bracken House on the day she'd called it off. Yet when he'd driven past that morning there had been no signs of life. But as he'd cruised along the main street of the village, luck had been with him. He'd seen Anna walking along the pavement with two small chidren.

If she'd been pleased to see him, Anna had concealed it well, he thought. Yet she'd gone to have a drink with him, invited him for a meal, and had agreed to see him again tomorrow. She seemed friendly enough but he sensed that she was on her guard for some reason and wondered if she thought it tasteless that he had resurfaced after all this time and was here in Willowmere.

Yet what did any of it matter? Unless she gave a sign that she still had feelings for him, he would accept that there really was nothing left of what they'd had before and go on his way.

'You're looking very glamorous,' Georgina said when Anna arrived at the surgery the following morning. 'What's the occasion?'

'Just afternoon tea with a friend I haven't seen for some time,' she replied.

Georgina Adams was an attractive thirty-five-year-old divorcee, who lived alone in a stone cottage at the end of one of the leafy lanes leading off the main street of the village. She kept herself to herself, but could be relied on for a cheery word and a smile whenever they stopped to chat.

The women patients usually chose to consult her, especially if they had something embarrassing to discuss, and she and James had a good working relationship.

Time was always of the essence on weekday mornings. Making sure the children had a good breakfast and seeing them safely to school before she put in an appearance at the surgery left little time for make-up and smart clothes. And in any case the practice nurses wore a neat blue uniform. But today she was wearing a fashionable cashmere top and skirt, and her hair hung straight and shining.

She'd decided that if Glenn didn't choose to join the practice it might be the last time she saw him, and whenever he thought of her in time to come, *if he ever did*, she wouldn't want him to remember her as drab.

All the practice staff, with the exception of herself, started at half past eight, so James and Georgina had already been seeing patients when she arrived, and Anna wondered when he was going to speak to Glenn.

She hoped it wouldn't be before they met up that afternoon. Calm and controlled was how she wanted to be while they walked by the lake and chatted over tea. The children were very good at the table, but Polly and Jolly were only five years old and sometimes they did need some assistance, which could prove to be a diverting exercise if a diversion was needed.

'I'm going to call at The Pheasant to see Glenn this evening when I've finished here,' James told her when he had a moment to spare. 'So I might be late for dinner. Is that all right?'

'Yes, of course,' she told him. 'I'll give the children theirs at the usual time, though.'

He nodded. 'And you're not going to say anything to Glenn about him joining the practice when you're with him this afternoon, are you?' he questioned.

'Absolutely not!' she exclaimed. 'I said last night that I don't want to be involved in what you are considering, James. I would be mortified if he received the impression that I had anything to do with it.'

'Don't be,' he said affectionately. 'You know I would never do anything to upset you. There's still time for you to say you would prefer me not to approach him.'

She shook her head. 'No. Go ahead. I think Glenn has been feeling rather out on a limb since he came back home. Your suggestion could be just what he needs.'

It was along the lines of what she'd been thinking during the sleepless hours of the previous night and as she went to change the dressing on what had been a badly infected finger of a teenage boy she still wasn't sure if it was what *she* needed.

The lad was the son of Bryan Timmins, who owned one of the biggest farms in the area, and until recently Anna had thought him to be spoilt and surly. When young Josh had pierced his finger on a rusty nail and it had become infected, James had put him on antibiotics and sent him to the nurses' room for a tetanus injection. Today she was hoping to see some improvement when she changed the dressing.

She'd seen a new side to Josh when he'd called at Bracken House one afternoon with some eggs that his father had forgotten to deliver and had stopped and played with the children.

They'd had lots of fun and Polly and Jolly hadn't wanted him to go, but his mother had phoned, concerned about where he'd got to, and he'd had to leave.

'How are the twins?' he asked as the finger was revealed and appeared to be healing satisfactorily.

'They're fine, Josh,' she replied. 'You're good with children, aren't you? I can see you having a house full of your own when you get married.'

'I don't know about that, but I won't have just one, *that's* for sure,' he said, and Anna saw the light. Josh had been a different person that day. He was obviously a lad who missed not having brothers and sisters.

'Come round any afternoon when you're not with your mates,' she said as he was leaving, and his expression brightened.

Georgina popped into the nurses' room shortly afterwards and said, 'I've just seen Josh Timmins leaving. That young man is in for a surprise and so are you, Anna.'

'Why me?' she asked.

'His mother came to see me yesterday afternoon and she will be attending our antenatal clinic in the morning.'

'Maggie Timmins is pregnant!' she exclaimed. 'That is amazing!'

'What do you mean? She's not exactly in her dotage,' Georgina protested mildly. 'Maggie was forty last month, which isn't exactly the first flush of youth but not too old to conceive.'

'That isn't what I meant. Another child in the family could make a big difference to Josh's life.'

'I know what you mean. Lots of teenagers don't take

kindly to finding out what their parents have been up to *and* the prospect of perhaps having their nose pushed out of joint.'

'That won't apply to Josh,' Anna informed her. 'From what I know of him, he'll be delighted. He loves children. You should see him with Polly and Jolly.'

'Anyone would love those two,' Georgina said wistfully, and aware that the dark-haired doctor was hurting for some reason, Anna let the subject drop.

'What is it to be first?' Glenn asked when she opened the door to him just minutes after she and the children had arrived home from school. 'Willow Lake or the Hollyhocks Tea Rooms?'

He'd exchanged the suit of the night before for the warm sweater and jacket, and instead of feeling tense at the sight of him Anna felt suddenly as if the sun had come out from behind a cloud.

He was smiling and she wondered if the smile would still be there when James put forward his proposition. But that was not on the menu at the moment and knowing that the children would be hungry she said, 'Let's eat first, shall we? It's the kind of day when one feels the need for something warm inside. It could be chilly by the water with the snow still around.'

'Did you say that the Hollyhocks place is near the post office?' he questioned as the three of them came trooping out to join him.

'Yes, we'll be there in minutes.' And with Pollyanna and Jolyon skipping along in front, they set off in that direction.

Anyone who didn't know them would think they

were a family, she thought, but they would be very much mistaken. It was a scenario she couldn't visualise in the near future, or the far distance for that matter, but Glenn was strolling along beside her contentedly enough and the old familiar ache was there.

After a delicious meal, Glenn sat back contentedly in his chair. 'That was fantastic food!' he said to Emma, the pleasant, middle-aged woman who came to clear the table. 'I can't remember when I last tasted anything so good, and the children have cleaned their plates too.'

Anna nodded, and smiled. 'Emma's husband, Simon, is the cook, and Emma rules the roost in here, don't you?'

'Yes, I suppose I do,' she agreed, 'but it's Simon's baking that brings the customers in.' She glanced at Glenn. 'We haven't seen you in these parts before. I take it you're a friend of Anna's.'

'We studied medicine in London at the same time some years ago,' he said. 'I was passing this way and called to see her.'

'Oh, yes, Simon and I saw you both in The Pheasant last night,' Emma said, and Anna guessed they would be thinking that she'd found herself a man. It was what she'd thought herself once but had discovered that the fates had had other plans and in spite of Glenn coming to seek her out she had no expectations of anything changing with regard to that.

As the four of them got up to go, the children hesitated with their bright blue gazes on Emma behind the counter. She smiled and, pushing a tray of freshly baked gingerbread men towards them, said, 'I haven't forgotten. Help yourselves, my dears.' As they promptly obeyed, she told Glenn, 'When Pollyanna and Jolyon come here they always get a gingerbread man to take home.'

'Nice people,' he said as they walked towards their destination. 'I couldn't see that happening in the cities. Getting to know one's neighbour is a rare happening.'

'So there are some nice things you will remember about Willowmere when you leave us?'

'Oh, yes, definitely, but I'm not all that sure my turning up on your patch has given *you* much pleasure. You seem to have a keen interest in my departure.'

'Not at all,' she protested, her colour rising, 'but when you go, don't forget that James will want to say good-bye.'

It was on the tip of her tongue to tell him that James had something to say that might make goodbyes fly out of the window, but she'd promised not to say anything, and in any case she wanted this time together to be free of tension.

'Wow!' he exclaimed as the lake suddenly appeared before them, cold and crystal clear beneath the slender drooping branches of the trees that had given it its name. 'What a heavenly place! Do you come here often?'

'As often as I can. James and I bring the children here for picnics in summer and sometimes if I have a spare moment I come to enjoy the silence on a summer evening. The willows are much greener then, but as you can see they retain some of their leaves in winter and are still very beautiful.'

'You love this place, don't you?' he said gravely. 'And I can understand why.'

She was smiling, hazel eyes bright with pleasure

because he understood how she felt about the lake, and she told him, 'When I want to be invigorated I walk by the river as it bustles along, but if I want peace I come here.'

'On your own? It sounds rather solitary.'

'It may be hard to understand but I've become a very solitary person, Glenn, even though I lead such a busy life.'

'Maybe it's because you put all your energies into the lives of others and need to shut down occasionally. That was how I used to feel sometimes when I was out there with a never-ending queue of people needing my help, and now I've come back it's just the opposite. Nobody needs me,' he said with a dry smile.

Anna was silent for a moment before she said levelly, 'I don't think any doctor can truthfully say *that*.'

'No. I suppose not,' he agreed, as a flock of Canada geese arose out of reeds by the lakeside and flew overhead in formation, silhouetted against a winter sunset. 'It's just that I'm not in the habit of lazing around, I suppose.'

The winter afternoon was closing in on them and, ready to change the subject, she said, 'We ought to be making tracks. It will be dark soon and it's getting colder.'

When they arrived back at Bracken House Glenn shook her hand. 'Goodbye, Anna,' he said. 'It's been great seeing you again. I've enjoyed meeting your brother and his beautiful children *and* seeing this place where you seem so content.'

*I thought I was*, a voice in her head suddenly whispered. She ignored it and told him, 'Yes, Willowmere is a lovely place. I'm surprised you don't want to see more of it. You'll call to say goodbye before you go, I hope.'

'Of course,' he said steadily.

It was half past six and he was a solitary figure in the dining room of The Pheasant when James appeared in the doorway. He rose to his feet but the other man waved him back down. 'Don't let me interrupt your meal,' he said. 'I'll ask the landlord to bring me a glass of wine.'

When that had been done James said, 'I wanted a word with you before you leave, Glenn.'

'Sure. What can I do for you?' he said easily.

'Would you be interested in a locum position at the practice?' James asked. 'We need another doctor now that Dad has passed on. It could be for as long as you wanted. If you decided to go back abroad or developed other plans, it would be fine by us. I've spoken to Georgina Adams, who is the other full time GP, and it's all right with her if you would consider joining us.'

Glenn had put his knife and fork down slowly. 'Yes, but what does Anna have to say?'

'The same as Georgina, that she has no objections.'

'She said that!'

'Yes, she did.'

'Then I'd like to take you up on your offer. A locum position was one of the things I'd been considering when I decided I was going to come back to the UK. You've solved that problem for me. It will be a pleasure to work with you, just as long as you're sure that Anna won't mind having me in the practice. Sometimes it's easier to work with strangers.'

'I discussed it with her before I approached you,' James assured him, 'and she said you would be an asset to the practice.'

'That's fine, then,' he said in disbelief. 'When do you want me to start?'

When James arrived home Anna and the children had just finished their meal and when she looked up from the table the question she was eager to ask was in the eyes meeting his.

'The answer is yes,' he told her. 'Glenn will be delighted to come into the practice. He's been thinking of doing something along those lines and when he'd satisfied himself that you would have no objections, he accepted my offer.'

'I see,' she said slowly, 'and you made it clear that it wasn't my idea.'

'Yes. He knows the suggestion is wholly mine. He's driving back to London early in the morning to tie up any loose ends there and will be back late Sunday night.

'When he mentioned accommodation I told him I have a spare room and he said that would be fine. It is fortunate he doesn't have a property to sell or anything. That sort of thing can drag on, and it's also fortunate that he likes us enough in Willowmere to stay for a while. I don't think we'll regret having him as part of the practice.'

After he'd eaten and gone upstairs to spend time with the children, Anna sat deep in thought. Everything was going to change and she had only herself to blame. If she'd said no when James had suggested asking Glenn to join them, she wouldn't be sitting around like a jelly with her confidence draining away like water down a drain.

When James had gone Glenn finished his meal and then went up to his room. He was smiling. The opportunity to stay in Willowmere was a gift from the gods. He hadn't wanted to return to London, but as a change of heart on Anna's part was not forthcoming there had seemed nothing else to do, short of outstaying his welcome.

But in the last hour everything had changed. He was filled with a renewed sense of purpose. If Anna didn't love him any more, and there was no reason why she should, at least they might become good friends.

She'd told him that she'd become a solitary person when she'd taken him to see the lake and he thought he understood. Her life was full of many things but they were the affairs of others, and there must be times when she was aware of that and felt alone.

She was surrounded by love, the giving and receiving of it, and unselfish and caring, would never accept that she was paying a price by putting to one side her own dreams and desires. Now he was back in her life, wondering if they could ever take up where they'd left off, longing to love and cherish her, but would she let him? He didn't think so and until Anna explained why she had sent him away on that dreadful day, nothing was ever going to make sense.

He arrived back from London late on Sunday evening and when he stopped the car in front of Bracken House its lights were shining out across what was left of the snow. As he sat looking around him for a moment he had the strangest feeling. It was like coming home, a sensation that he was not accustomed to.

In his young days 'home' had been anywhere his separated parents had been living at the time, and even now there was no reason for him to feel he belonged, but it was there nevertheless.

Anna's place next door was in darkness so it seemed that *she* wasn't around, but that didn't spoil the moment as he knew that she soon would be. They were going to be seeing each other all the time, at the surgery, here at Bracken House, and around the village.

Life was good and it became even better when she opened the door in answer to his ring on the bell. 'Hello, again,' she said coolly. 'I've been checking that all is in order for you, like clean towels in the en suite and fresh sheets on the bed.'

As she led the way into the kitchen she was aware that Glenn hadn't spoken so far, and the feeling of unreality that she'd had all day increased. She wasn't to know that the pleasure he'd felt out there in the car was still there and he was wallowing in it.

'How was the traffic?' she asked, and he eyed her blankly for a moment.

'Oh, all right,' he replied. In truth it had barely registered, so eager had he been to be where *she* was, but the cool greeting and the polite enquiry about the journey indicated that Anna hadn't exactly been glowing with anticipation, but he could cope with that. The main thing was that he was here in Willowmere to live. It was more than he had ever dreamed of and the fact that she had been in favour of it had given him new determination not to be side-tracked any more.

Unaware of the thoughts going around in his mind Anna was leading the way upstairs. Looking around him, he said, 'Is James not here?'

'No,' she replied. 'He's gone round to have a quick word with Elaine, the practice manager. He's so busy during the week there's no time for discussing admin-istration matters and they often communicate over the weekend. He said to tell you he won't be long and to make yourself at home.'

They were on the landing now and when she opened the door nearest to them he followed her inside.

'I hope you'll be comfortable in here,' she said, 'and feel free to call the rest of the house your home for however long you are here. James is looking forward to you staying here.'

No mention of her feelings on the matter, he noticed and his glance went to the double bed. Did Anna remember the times they'd slept together in blissful contentment after they'd made love? he wondered. He turned to face her and knew she was reading his mind.

He took a step towards her and she backed away. 'Don't!' she begged.

'Don't what?' he questioned in a low voice.

'Don't bring it all back. It's gone, Glenn,' she choked.

'I don't intend to,' he said in the same quiet tone, and looked around him. 'This is a charming room. Thanks for making it so. I shall look forward to enjoying the view from the window when daylight comes.'

Anna was already at the door and bringing the moment down to basics was asking, 'Have you eaten?'

'Yes, thanks, though I wouldn't mind a cup of tea.'

'Of course. I'll switch the kettle on.'

At that moment James returned. The two men were chatting when Anna appeared with two mugs of tea and when her brother asked why she wasn't joining them she made the excuse that she was leaving them to discuss Glenn's arrival at the practice and was going to have an early night.

'Sleep well,' she said to Glenn from the doorway, still in the role of the polite hostess, 'and don't bother to set an alarm. The cockerel at the farm down the road will waken you at an early hour, and if he doesn't the children will.'

'Magical! I'll remember that,' he said dryly, and James, seated beside him, laughed at his wry expression.

'I'll be off, then,' she told them, and as Glenn fixed her with his dark blue gaze she knew she hadn't been wrong about the way they'd been ready to gravitate towards each other in the bedroom. Thank goodness she'd had the sense not to weaken.

She wasn't going to get away so easily, though. He was on his feet and saying, 'I'll see you to your door,'

'It's only a few feet away!'

'Nevertheless.' He turned to James. 'I'll only be a matter of minutes.'

Her brother was smiling. The undercurrents he'd sensed on the night that Glenn had dined with them were still there. If not on Anna's part, they were certainly there on Glenn's.

'This is crazy!' she protested as they walked the few feet to her door.

'Yes, maybe,' he parried. 'As crazy as what happened up in the bedroom, do you think?'

'Nothing happened in the bedroom,' she protested flatly.

'Exactly, but it could have done.'

She was putting her key in the lock. 'It was over a long time ago, Glenn. Don't try and rake up the ashes.'

'Is that how you really feel?'

'Yes. I'm afraid so.'

He took a step back. 'Fair enough. Maybe one day you'll tell me what it's all about.'

'There's nothing to tell,' she said, pushing the door wide. 'Goodnight, Glenn.'

Anna's arrangement with James for weekday mornings ever since she'd moved into the annexe had been that he would get the children up and give them their breakfast, and once that was over she would come in to oversee Pollyanna and Jolyon getting washed and dressed and ready for school while he prepared to be at the surgery for half past eight.

The following morning would be the same, except that Glenn would be there, making his own preparations to accompany James. When she appeared he flashed a smile in her direction and she was relieved to see that it held no reminders of the night before. The same didn't apply to his thoughts, but she wasn't to know that.

In the midst of the hustle and bustle he said, 'To work with just the sounds of the countryside in my ears will be pure joy. And, Anna, I don't believe I thanked you last night for getting my room ready. It was remiss of me and my only excuse is that I had other things on my mind.'

She paused in the middle of supervising Jolyon tying the laces in his school shoes and looked up at him from a crouching position.

If Glenn thought she was going to take him up on that, he had another think coming. It was daunting enough having him around at this time of day without playing mind games, and she went to check that the children had everything they needed for school.

She'd woken up with the same kind of dread as when she had a dental appointment. The feeling that pain, or at least discomfort, lay ahead. But there was no time to dwell on what Glenn's first day in the practice was going to be like, she would know soon enough.

He was already settled in the room next to Georgina, when she arrived after taking Pollyanna and Jolyon to school, and was saying goodbye to his first patient of the day, Esther Whittaker, the oldest inhabitant of the village.

'I've seen some doctors come and go at this place in my time,' she was telling him with a wizened smile. 'I like to see a new face now and then so you'll be seeing a lot of me as I'm an old crock who is a regular visitor to this place.'

'I will bear that in mind, Mrs Whittaker,' he told her gravely as he saw her safely off the premises.

Bemused by the sight of crusty old Esther Whittaker eating out of his hand, and unable to resist commenting on it when he came back inside, Anna said, 'It hasn't taken you long to settle in.'

'Maybe it's because settling-in time was not on the agenda where I've been,' he said quizzically. 'The moment we stepped out of a helicopter, or put a foot on dry land if we'd used a boat to get to some far-away place, people were there, begging to be treated.'

She nodded sombrely. 'I *would* like to hear about it some time. It will be in the far distant future before I get the chance to do anything like that, but maybe one day. In the meantime, I make the most of my nurse's training by helping to look after the people here in Willowmere.' She glanced over at some new arrivals. 'I see a couple of them heading for the chairs in the passage outside the nurses' rooms, so I'll leave you, Glenn. I take it that you've been introduced to every-one.'

'Yes. James did the honours as soon as we arrived.'

'Where is he now?' she asked.

'He's with Elaine, sorting out final details of my function here with regard to the primary care trust. He seems to think that they won't need to be involved as I'm not here on a permanent basis.'

'No, of course not,' she said, and thought that now Glenn was actually here she didn't want to be reminded that it might not be for long.

'You've kept your friend Dr Hamilton to yourself, haven't you?' Beth teased as they prepared the bigger of their rooms for the heart clinic. 'I've only spoken to him briefly, but he's certainly going to brighten up our days while he's here.'

'We've only just renewed our acquaintance,' she told Beth. 'It's five years since I last saw Glenn and he *is* only a friend. He came to look me up and James saw the opportunity for some experienced help in the surgery.'

'Why? Where was he before?'

'Abroad, working with teams bringing health care to deprived areas.'

'That makes him more impressive than ever,' Beth said. 'A friend of my husband volunteered for that kind of thing and he said it takes a special kind of dedication for a person to do that.'

'Yes, I do know that,' Anna told her quietly, 'and I'm quite sure that Glenn will go back when he's had the chance to unwind.' She didn't really want to discuss him with Beth. Didn't want to be reminded of his zeal and idealism.

Compared to that she'd had just a single-minded determination to be there for those she loved and in the midst of it she'd lost the precious privilege of having children.

She didn't see Glenn much during the day. The two nurses were kept busy with those suffering from coronary problems who attended the heart clinic, checking blood pressures, sounding heartbeats, monitoring breathing and passing on details of any alarm signals to the doctors.

Only Georgina was around when Anna was on the point of going to collect the children in the afternoon and she said, 'James has taken Glenn with him on his house calls and he is about to find that in a country practice like ours the problem is not so much the number of patients as where they live. The distance between each call once away from the village can be very time-consuming. He seems a nice guy. I took him a coffee when I had mine in the middle of the morning.'

A wintry sun had been out and turned what was left of the snow to slush, and as she walked along Anna was thinking that if Glenn was going to be such a hit with the women on the staff, the low profile she intended to keep would be easier to achieve than she'd expected.

# CHAPTER FOUR

WHEN James came in at the end of the day he was smiling, and Anna asked, 'How did it go?'

'Very well indeed.' he replied. 'Glenn took to the surgery routine like a duck to water, and with regard to ducks and water he seems to have been impressed with his visit to Willow Lake. What prompted you to take him there in the middle of winter?'

'I suppose I was showing off. Keen for him to realise what a beautiful place this is.'

'Because now that he is here you want him to stay?'

'No. If you remember, I wasn't over the moon when you suggested bringing Glenn into the practice. My life is sorted, James. I don't want any complications in it and at the risk of Glenn becoming our main topic of conversation, what was he planning to do for his evening meal?'

'He's gone to the Hollyhocks for their last serving of the day.'

She smiled. 'That figures. He really enjoyed the food there when we went for afternoon tea.'

'If it's all right with you, I thought I'd invite him to eat with us each evening,' James suggested. 'He seems on top of the world to be here and, you never know, he might find himself a wife and become a permanent fixture.'

'Yes, he might,' she said with a sudden loss of appetite.

James received a phone call the next morning just as the two doctors were about to go to the surgery, and as he listened to what was being said at the other end Anna and Glenn watched his expression change.

'I'll go on ahead,' Glenn said.

She nodded as she heard James say, 'I'll be there as soon as I can, but first I will have to make some arrangements at this end.

'That was the nursing-home in Sussex where Julie's Aunt Alice has stayed for the past few years,' he explained when he'd finished the call. 'They rang to tell me that she died last night and as her executor I'm going to have to go to sort out funeral arrangements and deal with any other urgent matters that need attention.

'I hate to leave you to cope with the children, Anna, and am not happy about Glenn being thrown in at the deep end when he's only just joined us, but poor Alice had no living relatives, so I will have to go. Hopefully I'll find a hotel to stay the night and will be back late tomorrow. I'll go and speak to Georgina and then have a word with Glenn. It's going to mean you staying here tonight, so it's fortunate that he's going to be around. I'll be easier in my mind, knowing that you're not on your own with the children.'

'James!' she protested. 'I'm quite able to take care of myself and Polly and Jolly, so don't even think of asking Glenn to keep an eye on us. Right?'

'Right,' he agreed mildly, and went to find Georgina.

'No problem there,' he said when he came back. 'Both she and Glenn said not to worry so I'll go and pack an overnight bag and be off after I've said goodbye to the children.'

'Watch out for ice on the roads. There's still a lot of snow about too in some parts of the country,' she warned.

'Who's fussing now?' he wanted to know.

'Do I have to remind you that your children have already lost one parent in a car accident?'

'No, you don't,' he said sombrely. 'I will be careful.' He glanced at Polly and Jolly, who were dawdling around getting dressed. 'Thanks for this, Anna, especially at such short notice. I hate leaving you guys.'

'Yes, I know, but we'll be here when you get back,' she said gently. 'Have no worries about that.'

James had left, the children were dressed in their school uniforms and Anna had just come out of the shower when Glenn came back at just gone half past eight, bringing a gust of cold air in with him.

As she looked down at him from the upstairs landing, with a towel draped around her head and a warm robe loosely covering the rest of her, he said, 'Just a quick call to ask if there is anything I can do before I present myself to the waiting public.'

When she shook her head the towel fell off, and as she tried to retrieve it the robe nearly fell open.

He quickly turned away saying, 'Obviously the wrong time to call. I'm delaying you. Sorry about that.'

With the towel hanging loosely from one hand and

holding onto her dignity with the other, she said lightly, 'Thanks for the offer but everything is fine, Glenn. I'll catch up with you later.'

'Right. I'll be off, then,' he said, and went back to where he'd come from. As he closed the door behind him Anna thought that at one time they would have rolled about laughing at what had just happened with the towel.

But the clock was ticking on. It was time to dry her hair, put some clothes on and take the children to school, before presenting herself at the surgery.

'I've come for my B12 injection,' Melanie Bowers, a stressed-out mother of teenage sons, said when she presented herself at the nurses' room midmorning. 'I made an appointment yesterday.'

Beth was busy in the adjoining room, doing a spirometry test for someone with breathing problems, and Anna said, 'Come in and tell me what those boys of yours have been up to since I last saw you.'

'How much time have you got?' Melissa said, raising her eyes heavenwards. 'I thought it was hard work with three under five when they were little, but those days were a piece of cake compared to now!'

'You love them to bits, though, don't you?' Anna said as Melanie held out her arm for the injection.

She laughed. 'Yes, of course I do, but bear in mind what I say. Enjoy every moment with those two little darlings of yours. These are the easy years, Anna!'

Smiling, Anna put a plaster over the injection site, then said goodbye to Melanie. She went to the kitchen to make a coffee for Beth and herself, and as she passed the open door of Georgina's room she saw that the two doctors had had the same idea.

Glenn was perched on the corner of Georgina's desk with a mug in his hand and seated behind it the other permanent doctor in the practice was smiling across at him.

There was nothing wrong in what she was seeing, she told herself as she filled the kettle. The doctors always tried to manage a quick coffee some time during the morning, and if the two of them were enjoying getting to know each other, what was wrong with that?

Georgina would be a lovely woman to have for a friend if *she* had the time, but Glenn had all the time in the world and must see her as a pleasant diversion from an ex-girlfriend who was friendly one moment and un-approachable the next.

He'd seen her go by and on her return journey to the nurses' room was waiting for her in the passage.

'Need any help?' he asked as she stood before him with two mugs of coffee, adding, before she could reply, 'But I'm repeating myself. I've already asked that question once today and got nowhere. So I'd better let you pass before your coffee gets cold.'

'Yes, you had,' she said quietly, and went into her own domain.

Glenn and Georgina would make a striking couple, she thought as she drank the welcome brew. Both darkly attractive and free of commitments, as far as she knew. She felt like a pale-skinned, pale-haired nonentity by comparison.

James rang in the early evening to say he'd arrived safely and was already making the necessary arrangements. 'I'm hoping that the funeral can be arranged for Saturday so that I won't be missing from the surgery again,' he said, 'because I'll have to come back for it. Otherwise there will be no one there and I can't let that happen. Julie was very fond of her Aunt Alice. But it will mean leaving you with the children again, I'm afraid.'

'Just do what you have to do,' she told him, 'and here are your son and daughter to talk to you.'

When Glenn came in from the surgery she was standing at the cooker ready to serve the evening meal for herself and the children, and when he appeared in the kitchen doorway it was an awkward moment.

She didn't know whether James had done as he'd suggested and asked him to join them each day for their main meal and when he said, 'I've just stopped by to say I'm off to the Hollyhocks. I'll see you later,' she couldn't let him go foraging for a meal on a winter night when he'd been coping with extra pressures at the surgery all day in James's absence.

'I've made enough for four if you'd like to join us,' she said evenly. 'I know that James intended asking you to eat with us in the evenings while you're here.'

'And you don't mind?'

'No. It's as easy to cook for four as it is for three.'

'That wasn't what I meant. When I came to Willowmere I told you that it was for a short visit, but it hasn't turned out like that. I've taken employment with the practice and am living in what used to be your old home. To have you cook for me into the bargain is really too much to ask of you.'

'You aren't asking,' she told him chidingly. 'I'm offering. It's the least I can do.'

'You mean it is what politeness demands?' he questioned dryly.

A pan on the hotplate was threatening to boil over and as she adjusted the setting she said gently, 'Don't make something out of the offer that isn't there, Glenn. Shall we say it would be nice if you would join us?'

That brought a smile. 'Then I would be pleased to accept the offer.' As the four of them sat down together, Anna felt tears prick. It would be so easy to pretend they were a family, but the children belonged to someone else and every time she saw the man sitting opposite she had to remind herself that she'd sent him away once, and it was going to be a thousand times harder to do it a second time.

When the meal was over Pollyanna and Jolyon went upstairs to play until bedtime. Deprived of their childish chatter, the two adults sat in silence until Glenn said, 'So what sort of a day have you had, Anna?'

'Busy, as usual,' she said with a smile. 'Blood tests, injections, changing dressings, diabetes clinic first thing after lunch and the rest, but it is I who should be asking you that. James wasn't happy at leaving you on only your second day in the practice.'

'Neither of you need fret about that,' he said easily. 'I'm enjoying every moment of it. It's the nearest I've ever been to proper family life and I'm loving it.'

Don't, she begged silently. Glenn had no idea how much it hurt to hear him say that and how much it confirmed that she'd done the right thing all that time ago. Without making any comment, she got to her feet and began to clear away.

He was beside her in an instant. 'I'll do that while you're seeing to the children's bedtime. I'm a lodger, not a guest, and I haven't come to your village to muscle in on your life. I came for one last time before I sort out the rest of *my* life, and now I'm here I think I have my answer. I can see that if others need me, you don't.'

Pollyanna and Jolyon came running downstairs at that moment and Glenn sighed. Was he ever going to get an answer from Anna in words? he wondered. It was there in her actions but he wanted to know what the score was from her own lips.

'If you don't need me for anything, I'll go to the pub when I've done the dishes,' he said above the noise that the children were making. She nodded, relieved that they weren't going to be closeted together all evening.

It was ten o'clock and there was silence in the house. The children were asleep, but it had taken Jolyon longer than usual to settle down. He'd been fretful and kept wanting James, and it had taken Polly, who was a loving child, to console him by letting him hold her teddy as well as his own. He'd eventually gone to sleep holding a bear in each arm.

Anna had heard Glenn go out while she'd been supervising bathtime and thought she didn't blame him for going to the pub for some cheerful company. There weren't many laughs to be had at Bracken House when she was around.

She decided to have an early night and once she'd undressed she went down for a last hot drink before going to bed. As she sat by the fire sipping it slowly, Anna heard Jolyon coughing up above.

It was a harsh, grunting sort of bark, as if his airway was blocked, and she was up the stairs in a flash.

He was awake and the moment she reached the side of his bed she could see that he had a temperature. His brow was glistening with sweat, his cheeks bright red, and at that moment, woken up by the noise of his coughing, Polly, frightened by the sound, began to cry.

'Shush, Polly,' Anna said gently as she raised him up off the pillow. 'Jolly's just got a cough. He'll be all right in a moment.'

But she was not to be comforted and her crying grew louder as Anna loosened his pyjamas and tried to soothe him into letting her see down his throat, but he wouldn't let her and the dreadful coughing continued until she thought he was going to choke.

She was afraid to take her eyes off him, but if it was croup, and it sounded like it, Jolyon needed to be in a warm steamy atmosphere to ease the membranes of his throat. Propping him beside the bed in an upright position, she ran into the bathroom, grabbing a couple of towels and soaking them under the tap.

As she was hurrying back across the landing to drape the wet towels over the radiator she heard Glenn come in and shouted down the stairs, 'Glenn! Thank God you're back! I need your help.'

He came up the stairs two at a time, exclaiming, 'What a racket! Whatever is wrong with the children?'

'I think Jolly has got croup and Polly is frightened by the noise he's making,' she said.

'It does sound like croup,' he agreed, above the noise of Polly's sobs and Jolyon's coughing. 'Do I take it that it came on suddenly?'

'Yes, out of the blue, and suppose it isn't croup. That it's…' She couldn't put what she was thinking into words. It was too frightening.

'What?'

'Diptheria! The symptoms are similar at the onset,' she choked as she spread the wet towels over the radiator. She knew she was overreacting but the cold hand of dread was upon her heart.

Glenn was already carrying Jolyon to sit beside the radiator and reassuring him gently at the same time, and as the towels began to give off steam the coughing started to ease and Polly's sobs weren't quite so loud.

'Surely the children have been vaccinated?' he said.

'Yes, of course they have, but suppose it didn't take effect for some reason.'

'Anna, don't torture yourself. It's croup. I saw a child at the surgery this afternoon of a similar age to Jolyon and she had it. It's infectious, as we both know, so most likely they'll have picked it up at school. Keep your fingers crossed that Polly doesn't get it. Look, you can see the humidity is bringing relief and now that Polly is calming down, he's breathing more easily.'

His manner was reassuring, cool and matter-of-fact, and Anna would have been amazed if she'd known how he longed to take her in his arms and tell her not to worry, that he was there and always would be if she would let him.

If only he hadn't been so full of his own plans and ambitions when they'd graduated. If only the children's mother hadn't been taken from them, if only… He could go on for ever recounting his regrets, but what use would it be? The pattern had been set and it looked as if Anna wasn't ever going to budge from it.

'I wasn't expecting you back yet,' she said as she gave the children a drink before settling them down again. Jolyon's temperature was more normal now that the coughing had stopped, and she was hoping that soon they would be fast asleep again. But there would be no sleep for her in case there was a repeat of what had just happened.

'I only went because I didn't want to be in the way, but I'd had enough after a couple of drinks,' Glenn explained. 'Would you have phoned to ask for help if I hadn't arrived at that moment?'

'There hadn't been time. It all happened so quickly,' she told him, avoiding his glance. 'But you were a most welcome sight when you appeared.' Her voice thickened. 'I thought he was going to choke, Glenn. How would I have explained *that* to James?'

He held out his arms and said softly, 'Come here, my poor frantic one.' And as if some unseen force was controlling her movements, she went into them, unable to stop herself.

All she needed at that moment was comfort, he thought as he stroked her hair gently and pressed his lips against her brow. It was far from being an occasion for anything else and he was grateful that he was there to offer it.

But suppose he hadn't been present. There must have been countless occasions when she'd needed someone to be there for her besides James with his busy life. Yet it seemed that she hadn't wanted him, Glenn, to be the one, and she didn't seem to have found anyone else to fill the gap. He would dearly like to know what went on in Anna's mind.

'Go to bed,' he said as she withdrew herself from his hold, but she shook her head.

'I'm concerned that I mightn't hear Jolyon if he has another attack.'

'I'll stay up just to be on the safe side. I'll find a book and settle myself in a chair beside the bed.'

'I can't let you do that!'

'Oh, yes, you can.' He gave her a gentle push. 'Away with you, I promise I will come for you if he needs you. OK?'

'Yes, all right, and thanks for everything, Glenn.'

With his deep blue gaze darkening, he told her, 'I'm just happy to have been there for you and the children. No thanks are necessary.'

She nodded and as she went slowly to her room she was fighting the urge to go back to the warmth of his arms.

The rest of the night passed uneventfully. Anna slept fitfully and once when she went to the children's room to check on them she found Glenn observing her from his bedside vigil.

'Everything is fine,' he said in a low voice as she looked down at them. 'I was going to make a drink. Do you want one?'

'Yes,' she replied, and they went noiselessly downstairs together.

While they were waiting for the kettle to boil he went across to the window and looked out into the winter night where the village lay dark and still.

'It's only a short time to Christmas,' he remarked. 'I suppose it's pretty dead here and most people leave the village for their festivities.'

Anna turned away to hide a smile. 'We get by,' she told him. 'The farmers are always glad of help with plucking the turkeys, or there's following the gritting truck to make sure they don't miss anywhere, and if we want to do something really exciting, we tidy up the graveyard.'

He was laughing. 'All right, I get the message. Maybe I should wait and see.'

'Yes,' she told him. 'Maybe you should. Have you brought anything suitable for a black-tie affair?'

'No. Should I have?'

She didn't answer, just smiled across at him, and knew she was happy that for once at Christmastime Glenn would be where she could see him, touch him even.

As he poured the tea she said, serious once more, 'There will be two of us absent from the surgery tomorrow unless I bring Jolyon with me, as he won't be going to school, but I don't really want to do that. He needs to be kept away from any other infections.'

'We'll manage,' he told her. 'If James gets home tonight, he'll be back on the job tomorrow.'

She was feeling comfortable in his company for the first time since he'd come back into her life, Anna thought, and this was how she wanted it to stay. Maybe it would if she could only relax and stop fretting about what was and what wasn't happening.

'You've been a true friend tonight,' she told him. 'I'm sure you weren't expecting to be asked to join the surgery and spending the night on a chair watching over a sick child when you arrived in the uneventful countryside.'

He smiled a lopsided smile. 'You're not going to let me forget that, are you?'

She managed a smile of her own. 'With regard to Christmas, I should warn you that we have lots of holly and mistletoe around the surgery at Christmas and some of the staff can be women of strong passions.'

'But not you?' he questioned quizzically, while groaning inwardly at being described as merely a friend.

'No. Not me. I find life to be much simpler without them.'

He wasn't going to fall into any more traps of his own making so he didn't reply to that. But it didn't stop him from remembering, as he'd done a thousand times, that when he'd known her before she'd been a sweet, joyous thing in his arms when they'd made love.

It was coming up to six o'clock and he got to his feet in the cosy kitchen. He wasn't sure if his relationship with Anna had moved on during the night or taken a step back, but whatever it was there was time, he thought, lots of it, and Christmas was coming. If he had to resort to the mistletoe, he would hold her in his arms again somehow.

A knock on the front door announced a farmer delivering a chicken and some eggs, and when Bryan Timmins saw Anna he said, 'Hello, there, Anna. Have you heard I'm going to be a dad again? Talk about life begins at forty! Our young Josh is tickled pink, which is surprising for a lad of his age.'

'Yes, I've heard about the baby, Bryan,' she told him with a smile. 'Congratulations! And Josh is really good with children—you should see him with Polly and Jolly.'

He nodded. 'Aye, I know. His mother and me are sorry we haven't given him some brothers or sisters that would have been nearer his own age. But she had a bad time when Josh was born and this is a midlife surprise that we weren't expecting.'

'Josh?' Glenn questioned when the farmer had gone on his way.

'He's sixteen years old and a lovely lad. I'm very fond of him.'

'I see,' he said, and thought there was love in abundance in Anna's life. She'd had love for him once, but it hadn't lasted and there were no indications that it was going to be rekindled.

Glenn had left for the surgery, promising to ring at lunchtime to see how Jolyon was doing, and Anna phoned James to let him know what had happened.

'I am so sorry not to have been around when one of the children was poorly,' he said heavily. 'Thank goodness Glenn was there with you. I hope he isn't feeling that he is too near us for comfort.'

'I don't think you need fret about that,' she told him, 'or the fact that they're going to be you and I short at the surgery. He said not to worry. I suppose that what to us is a cause for concern will seem just a minor hiccup, compared to what he's been used to.

'Yet he didn't treat Jolyon as if it was something and nothing last night. He was calm and gentle, knew he was frightened *and* had to reassure me into the bargain as, although croup is bad enough, my imagination was running riot.'

'He's a good man,' James said approvingly, and Anna silently agreed. After chatting a little more, he told her he would be leaving for home mid-afternoon and rang off.

* * *

Glenn's first patient of the day was a newcomer to the village like himself. Alex Graham had moved into a flat above the antique shop, his intention being to paint the attractions of the Cheshire countryside, which were not in short supply.

The River Goyt and Peak Forest Canal ran side by side in rural splendour through the village. Willowmere was an artist's dream with its limestone cottages and shops that were far removed from the mass-produced, packaged image of the supermarket. But for any aspiring artist the lake, tranquil and ageless amongst the graceful trees after which it had been named, was always top of the list.

'I take it that you're here about the test results,' Glenn said as the lean, long-haired, thirty-plus patient seated himself opposite him.

'Yeah,' he said. 'I've been visiting relatives and when I got back late last night there was a message on my answering machine to say that the results of the tests I've been having had arrived and that the surgery wanted to discuss them with me.'

Glenn nodded. 'Yes, that is so. I'm sorry to inform you that the pain and inflammation of your joints is caused by the onset of rheumatoid arthritis.'

'Hell!' he groaned. 'If I can't paint I'll either starve or die of boredom.'

'That is the bad news,' Glenn told him. 'The upside of it is that it can be treated with non-steroidal, anti-inflammatory medicines to relieve the stiffness and pain, and drugs like gold penicillin will arrest the progress of the illness. Then, as in all complaints of this nature, there is physiotherapy to fall back on.'

'Whatever you say,' Alex said dejectedly. 'Just as long as I can use my hands.'

'We should be able to do more than that for you once we've got you on the right treatment,' Glenn told him. 'James Bartlett, the senior partner, isn't here at the moment, but he has left instructions, so think positive, Alex.'

As his patient nodded bleakly Glenn said on a lighter note, 'I had time to kill when I arrived in the village last week and saw a watercolour of Willow Lake that you'd done on display in the window of the picture gallery near the church. It was on the same day that Anna Bartlett, one of the practice nurses, had taken me to see her favourite place and I recognised it at once. I'm no expert but I thought it very good, and having met the artist I'm interested in buying it for her.'

Alex was cheering up by the minute. 'That would be great. It will keep the wolf from the door so to speak. I've had no word from Clare, who owns the gallery, to say that it's been sold, so it should still be available. Guess what? I'm feeling better already!'

'And you'll feel better still when you start on the treatment,' he told him as he printed out the necessary prescriptions.

# CHAPTER FIVE

WHEN Alex Graham had gone Glenn saw that the first signs of Christmas were appearing in Willowmere. Workmen from the council were erecting a large spruce tree in the centre of the village green and he thought that it would be the first time ever he hadn't felt alone at Christmas. He would be near Anna, James and the children, only on the edge of their lives maybe, but there nevertheless.

He rang to ask how Jolyon was before setting off on his rounds and Anna said, 'He's rather pale and listless and occasionally the barky cough appears, but nothing like it was in the night.'

'And Pollyanna, how is she?' he asked. 'Are there any signs that she might be sickening for the croup?'

'Not so far. I'm still keeping the atmosphere moist and in a few moments am going to give the children their lunch. I've spoken with James and he should be home some time this evening, so hopefully we won't be disturbing you tonight.'

'I was going to say it was a pleasure,' he remarked, 'but there is no pleasure in watching over a sick child. I'm just glad I was around when I was needed, that's all.'

'So am I.'

'What?'

'Glad you were around when I needed you.'

'It felt good to be needed by you,' he said quietly.

Confused, Anna opened her mouth to reply but before she could speak he said, 'Sorry. Forget I said that. Take care, Anna. I'll see you whenever.'

His call, made from the best of intentions, left her feeling off balance and low of spirits, but she told herself that if Glenn was going to be around for some time, she was going to have to get used to those sorts of feelings.

When James arrived home the children had just gone to bed and the first thing he did was to go straight upstairs to check on Jolyon, before tucking them up for the night.

'How has he been, Anna?' he asked when he came down. 'Jolly looks a bit washed out and is hoarse due to the coughing, but the lymph glands in his neck aren't up and he seems cool enough.'

'He hasn't been too bad since last night,' she told him. 'The coughing comes and goes. So far Polly hasn't shown any signs of croup, but Glenn said he'd seen a child at the surgery yesterday who had it, so it would seem that it is going around the school.'

'Yes. You're probably right, and now I'm going to have a word with him. There's a light on so I take it that he's in his room. I need to know if there have been any problems at the surgery while I've been away. I won't be long and when I come back if you want a break from me and mine, by all means have one.'

'There's a meeting in the village hall at eight o'clock to sort out the arrangements for the various Christmas activities, and I'd like to be there,' she replied, 'but first tell me about the funeral arrangements you've been making for Aunt Alice. When is it to take place?'

'Saturday, as I had hoped, and there will just be myself and a couple of the staff from the home present. It will mean me being away overnight again, but that will be the end of it. Any other matters regarding her estate I can deal with from home.'

When he came back from seeing Glenn she was ready to go to the meeting and he said, with the practice still in mind, 'It seems that everything has been in control at the surgery. It's been pretty busy, as it is at this time of the year but he and Georgina have coped. Glenn said that Alex Graham has been in for his test results and was pretty devastated, being an artist, but he sorted him out and the guy went on his way feeling more cheerful than when he'd arrived.' He gave her a gentle push. 'And now away with you, and don't rush back.'

'I'll see,' she said, and after closing the door behind her hurried down the garden path en route for the village hall, with eyes averted from the lighted room above where Glenn was to be found.

When she heard the front door of the house open and close behind her she stopped, turned, and he was there, striding towards her dressed in a sweater and jeans and saying, 'I'm going to post a letter.' His glance took in the long winter coat she was wearing. 'It would seem that you're going further afield than that. Where are you off to?'

'I'm going to a meeting in the village hall about Christmas events,' she explained. 'It starts at eight o'clock.'

'I see.' He pointed to the big spruce in the middle of the village green that the council had erected and which was as yet bare of any decorations. 'That being the first reminder, I take it.'

'Yes, it is,' she agreed, 'and tonight we will be arranging a candlelit service in the church on Christmas Eve, with some of us going carol singing afterwards, *and* a Mistletoe Ball, just to name a few of our Christmas traditions.'

'Sounds impressive,' he commented, 'and a fitting answer to me thinking Willowmere would be dead during the festive season. Can anyone come?'

'Where to, the carol singing, the candlelight service or the ball?'

'I was referring to the meeting.'

'Er, yes, but are you sure?' she questioned, taken aback at the request, but with pleasure surfacing at the thought.

'Yes. I've nothing else planned for this evening. I'll have to pop back inside for a jacket, though. I was only expecting to go as far as the post office.'

As they retraced their steps he said, 'Are you coming back inside? I'll only be a moment but it is too cold to be standing around outside.'

She nodded, having just remembered a list of volunteers for various things that she needed to take with her, and followed him upstairs. His bedroom door was wide open as he reached into the wardrobe and when she looked into the room her eyes widened.

There was a photograph of the two of them on top of a chest of drawers. It had been taken by a student friend of Glenn on his graduation day and it was easy to see that the two in the picture were in love. She had a similar one that had been taken on *her* graduation day, but she hadn't been able to look at it after she'd sent him away and it had been at the bottom of a drawer ever since.

If he'd deliberately left it out, he must have been aware that sooner or later she would see it. So what was the idea? Was he playing mind games after promising not to intrude into her life? She wished she knew, but it would have to be another time when she mentioned it. He was coming out of the bedroom and she thought wryly that she didn't want to spoil the evening ahead. Every moment was precious.

The meeting was always chaired by the vicar and was usually a gathering of brains, brawn, organising ability and creative talent. The first person they saw when they arrived was Alex Graham, the artist, and then others began to arrive.

As the vicar opened the proceedings he remarked that they were pleased to see two newcomers amongst them in the form of Dr Glenn Hamilton, who had recently joined the GP practice, and Alex Graham, a talented artist. She couldn't believe this was happening, Anna thought. Glenn, who'd been more of a town and city person when she'd known him before and had teased her about her love of Willowmere, was involving himself in village affairs.

James had been watching through the sitting-room window as Anna had left the house and when Glenn had appeared simultaneously he'd smiled a satisfied smile. He'd caught sight of the photograph when he'd gone to talk to Glenn, had drawn his own conclusions and commented that he couldn't stay long as Anna was on the point of going out.

He hadn't known whether the ploy would work but it had, and it proved that his instinct regarding the two of them was right. He sensed the attraction between them every time they were together, but with regard to Anna especially he doubted whether she would ever admit it because of the role she played in his own life, and then there was that other matter that she never referred to but which he knew must be a constant source of anguish.

Yet she was entitled to a life of her own, a husband of her own, and children, if not biological children, still little ones to love. He cared for her too much to ever want her to miss out on those things. It was Anna's own sense of duty that was keeping her with him and the children.

So far he had let her persuade him that she was content, but he had promised himself that if ever she met the man of her dreams he would see to it that she didn't let love pass her by because of family ties. Maybe Glenn Hamilton was that man, but only time would provide the answer to that.

When they came out of the meeting into the cold December night Glenn said, 'You don't have to go straight home, do you?'

'Not if I don't want to.'

'So maybe we could call in at the Pheasant?'

'Yes, why not?' she agreed, and pushed to one side the thought that the more time she spent with Glenn the harder it was going to be to convince him that nothing had changed.

He could see her face in the light of a streetlamp and thought of the number of times he'd brought it to mind while he'd been away, and now that Anna was actually here beside him he felt as far away from her as he had then.

Yet she was smiling now as she said, 'You know, James is really pleased to have you in the practice, and so is Georgina.'

'I note there is no mention of *your* feelings on the subject,' he remarked dryly.

'I was the one who recommended you, if you remember.'

She could have told him that as well as the vote of confidence she'd felt that having him in the practice was better than nothing, which was what she'd had for a long time.

As they seated themselves at one of the tables in the Pheasant she said, 'I would have thought you might want to spend Christmas somewhere more upmarket.'

'What, and miss all the goings-on in the village?' he teased, and then became serious again. 'I intend to be *here*. I can't think of anywhere I would rather be, but I don't want to foist myself onto you and James and the children. It will be sufficient just to be near.'

Anna felt tears prick and, not wanting him to see them, turned away. What had they come to? she thought. That Glenn, who'd always been the vibrant, confident one, should be content just to be on the fringe of their Christmas celebrations. She knew that even if it turned out to be a painful pleasure, she wanted him there.

'You are welcome to share our Christmas,' she told him. 'It's a magical time here in Willowmere and I would hate you to be alone.'

'It wouldn't be the first time if I was.'

'I know. That was then. This is now, and I don't want to think any further than that. Can't we just have a lovely Christmas together?'

'Yes, if that is what you want,' he said levelly, thinking that it would be another memory to add to the list, if nothing else.

They had just the one drink and then Glenn said, 'I think I should take you home after you having had so little sleep last night.'

Anna nodded in reluctant agreement. She could have stayed there for ever, but there was no telling what turn the conversation might take and she had to admit that she *was* tired.

So they went out once more into the winter night where the lights of Bracken House were shining out across the village green, and she wished that it was the two of them returning to a home of their own.

'I don't think we'll be disturbed tonight,' she told him. 'Jolyon seems much better and James is back, so I can return to my own place tomorrow, but he's going to be away again on Friday night as it's the funeral on the Saturday.'

They went upstairs together, each to their separate rooms, and as he opened the door of his bedroom she could see the photograph again. Following her glance he said, 'Do you remember us having that taken?'

'Yes, of course I do. I'm surprised to find it on display, though.'

'Why? After being sent packing it was something to remind me of you. I haven't seen yours on view but, then, I suppose it wouldn't be as you were so keen to make a clean break.'

'So didn't you have any other relationships during that time?' she asked, steering the conversation in another direction that might prove just as personal.

'No,' he replied, observing her with raised brows.

'Not even for ease of the body?'

'No. I had neither the time nor the inclination. What about you?'

'With two small children needing me I didn't have the time either for the kind of thing we're talking about.' She paused, listening. 'Judging from the silence that prevails at this moment, they are both fast asleep and their father, too, from the sound of it.'

She sounded chirpy enough, he thought, but Anna was very pale and, touching her cheek gently, he said, 'Goodnight, Anna. Thanks for letting me into your life again for a little while.'

Rendered speechless by the tenderness in his voice, she nodded, turned blindly and went into her bedroom, closing the door slowly behind her.

She should be avoiding those sorts of moments, she thought as she threw herself on top of the covers. The temptation to tell Glenn the truth was overwhelming on such occasions.

Why had he come back after all this time? she asked herself. Was it out of curiosity to see what she'd done with her life while he'd been away, and on finding that it didn't amount to much had decided to stay around for a while?

Since he'd come back she'd become aware of his loneliness and was happy that in some small way she and James, with his offer of employment, were making Glenn feel at home in Willowmere.

She still had to pinch herself when she thought of how he'd settled into the practice with a minimum of fuss and was obviously enjoying rural health care, *and* that he was impressed with the lake. Most surprising of all was that he was only feet away across the landing.

Maybe she should be counting her blessings and accepting him as a friend, but she realised now that she was beginning to want more than that, and it just wasn't going to happen.

She heard the church clock strike twelve and, turning her head into the pillow drifted off into shallow sleep.

By the time James was ready to drive to Sussex again in the late afternoon of Friday, Jolyon had recovered from the croup and so far Pollyanna had not succumbed.

The moment he'd arrived home earlier in the week he had ordered a humidifier to be delivered to replace the makeshift arrangement with the towels, and it seemed to be working.

Unless Polly started with the croup over the weekend, Anna would be back on duty at the practice on the coming Monday, and she was looking forward to it.

She enjoyed working as a practice nurse, even though she'd had her sights set on something higher when she'd been at university. But she was sensible enough to realise that combining the two, working at the surgery and being there for the children when James wasn't around was an arrangement that couldn't be bettered.

At the practice she and Beth got on well. The older woman was always willing to hold the fort if she needed to be with Pollyanna and Jolyon, as had been the situation over the last couple of days.

Anna also had a good relationship with Georgina workwise, but the attractive doctor kept her private life very much under wraps and Anna felt that somewhere along the line she had known grief of some kind, like James and herself…

Elaine, the practice manager, was efficiency personified, with a degree in business management, and frowned upon anyone who interfered with the smooth running of the village's health-care arrangements.

Single and, as far as Anna knew, not in any kind of relationship, Elaine was a petite blonde in her late forties with a flair for design as well as an orderly mind. She was always active in bringing the joys of Christmas to the village and had been at the meeting the other night.

So when Monday came Anna would be teaming up once more with the three that she was closest to at the surgery, but before Monday there was the weekend to get through. Most of the time James would be away and she felt down in the dumps.

On Friday night the children had had their baths and were sitting clean and rosy-cheeked, drinking their bedtime milk, when Glenn appeared in the kitchen.

'How about I make us a late supper?' he suggested.

'I thought you might be glad of some company when Pollyanna and Jolyon have gone to bed, even if it's only me.'

What was she supposed to say to that? Anna wondered and knew there was only one thing *to* say. 'Well, OK, that would great,' she told him, trying to ignore the butterflies in her stomach at the thought of an evening alone with him.

He'd bought steaks to eat with salad, a sherry trifle from the confectioner's next to the post office, and a bottle of wine to go with them, and when she'd set the table with the best china and lit candles, Anna went upstairs to change out of the jeans and T-shirt she was wearing.

She came down again in a long black skirt, a cream silk top and a beautiful gold necklace that had been her mother's, and was hoping that Glenn wouldn't think it was a bit over the top for an unexpected supper. She'd given in to the urge to look beautiful for him, as at that moment all her intentions to be aloof had been put on hold.

'Wow!' he said when she appeared beside him at the cooking range. 'Dare I hope that you've dressed up for me?'

'It's nice to make an effort sometimes,' she told him lightly. 'Apart from at the surgery, when I'm in my uniform, I spend a lot of time in jeans and a T-shirt, and it can get to be too much of a habit.'

'Yes, I'm sure it can,' he said mildly as he uncorked the wine, 'and now, if madam would like to take a seat, sir will bring in the food.'

As they sat facing each other across the dining table

he raised his glass, and as she looked into his dark blue gaze he said, 'To you, Anna, in all your many guises, stand-in mother, sister in a million, practice nurse…and friend. I wish you much happiness in the life you've chosen.'

She put down her glass. 'I didn't choose it,' she told him in a low voice. 'It chose me, but, please, don't let's go into that. Can't we talk about something else?'

'Yes, of course,' he agreed, as if it was of no consequence and said jokingly, 'How about the surgery for a fresh topic of conversation? Do you want to hear what's been happening there today in your absence?'

'What I don't know about I won't be anxious about so, no,' she told him, matching his change of mood. 'Just as you won't want to know what's been happening in my day.'

'How do you know I won't?' he said in a low voice, and it was there again in the quiet room, the chemistry between them that hadn't gone and never would as far as she was concerned.

To bring normality back to the atmosphere Anna reached across the table for a helping of salad to go with the steak, and as she did so the sleeve of her dress, which fanned out at the wrist, wafted towards one of the candles.

'Watch out!' he cried, and as she looked up, startled, he gripped her arm and pulled it away from the naked flame. 'That could have been serious,' he said, without removing his hold. Getting to his feet, he came round to her side of the table.

As she looked up at him questioningly he raised her to her feet and when they were facing each other he said,

'You almost set yourself on fire a moment ago, Anna. Are you trying to give me a heart attack?'

He bent and blew out the candles, leaving the room in shadow with the only light coming from the fire burning brightly in the grate. And as their glances held he murmured, 'I know it's against the rules that you've laid down, but I feel I'm entitled to this.'

Before she could speak she was in his arms. He was kissing her with an urgency that was setting her on fire, and as she responded to his arousal the desert that was her heart became a green and pleasant place.

But she couldn't let it go on, she thought frantically as he lifted his head and, looking deep into her eyes, traced his fingers across the lips that he'd just kissed.

'So you *do* still care,' he said softly.

'Yes! No! We can't!' she gasped, and pointed to the table. 'This was a mistake. I've told you before, Glenn, don't complicate my life.'

'Is that really how you feel?' he asked flatly as his arms fell away.

'Yes.'

'All right. I'm sorry.'

'Don't leave in anger!' she pleaded as he moved towards the door. 'Don't leave the village because of me!'

He turned and observed her unsmilingly. 'I'm not going anywhere yet.' He turned and went slowly up the stairs.

Well done! Glenn told himself grimly as he closed the bedroom door behind him. What about the patience that you promised yourself, the promises to keep your distance? You've just shown yourself to be a man of his word, *I don't think*!

He turned at the sound of hurrying footsteps coming up the stairs and when he opened the door to her knock he found Anna with a plateful of the food he'd prepared. Before he could say anything she said awkwardly, 'The steak is still warm and the salad crisp.'

She saw him frown and said quickly, 'Don't refuse it, Glenn, or you'll make me feel even worse than I do already.' And thrusting the plate into his hand, she hurried back to where she'd come from.

If it wasn't so sad it would be funny, he thought as he looked down at the congealing meat. Anna following him with the remains of the meal, begging him to eat it, when right now he felt as if it would choke him.

Anna lay in bed, unable to sleep. Despite the evening ending badly, it had shown her something that scared and thrilled her at the same time. The magic was still there and as strong as ever. That kind of kissing had always led to them making love in that other life when everything had been so simple. Now it was far from that, which was why she'd called a halt.

Tomorrow James would be home again and then maybe they could get back into their safe, secure routine and Glenn would find better things to do with his time than spending it with her.

For one thing, they wouldn't be continually in each other's space. She would be back next door and they would only meet up at the surgery.

There was no sign of him when she got up on Saturday morning and his car wasn't parked outside so she presumed he must have gone into the city to do some shopping. She decided that she and the children would do likewise, but in another direction.

They would go for a Christmas tree to the place where her parents before her had always gone, to a farm high up on the road that led to the moors and the peaks beyond.

'James's young 'uns aren't half shootin' up, Anna,' Bill Bradshaw, who owned the farm, said as he took them to select a tree. 'It doesn't seem long since he brought you home from the hospital with the babies one on either side of you. I remember the wife cried buckets.'

'Yes, I know,' she told him. 'Everyone was wonderful. Bringing food, taking the washing and bringing it back ironed, as well as lots of other kindnesses that showed how people here look out for each other.'

'Aye,' he agreed. 'Everybody rallies round when one of our own is havin' it rough. The bush telegraph does overtime. Gettin' back to this tree that you've come for, I take it you want a big 'un.'

'Yes, a big tree for a big room.'

When she'd made her choice he said, 'I'll drop it off for you in a couple of hours if that's all right. So what's this I hear about a new doctor at the surgery? I hope James isn't thinkin' of leavin' us.'

'No, nothing like that,' she assured him. 'Glenn Hamilton has been working abroad and has come as locum for a while.'

'I see,' he said, and without batting an eyelid he added, 'I was askin' because I've got a man's problem and I'd rather see that brother of yours or this new fellow than Georgina Adams, sweet girl though she is.'

'You'll be fine with either of them but, Bill, don't wait too long to make an appointment. All things that worry us healthwise should be dealt with promptly, and if we are told there is no cause for alarm we can relax all the sooner. Or if it should turn out to be the opposite then there will have been no delay in getting treatment.'

As they drove back down the hillside Anna saw that Glenn's car was following them down and they pulled up outside the practice at the same time. There was an awkward pause as they faced each other and she broke the silence by saying stiltedly, 'I thought you might have gone into town to shop.'

He shook his head. 'No. I've been for a drive around the surrounding countryside, getting my bearings, and have decided that it's a bit bleak up there in winter. Do the doctors get called out much to those parts?'

'Sometimes. My dad was once trapped up there over-night in a blizzard when he'd been to visit a patient. He had to stay in his car until the snow ploughs cleared the way for him the following morning. The children and I would have taken you around the places that you need to get to know if you'd said,' she informed him. 'You had only to ask.'

'What? After last night?' he said dryly. 'I don't want to put my foot in it twice. By the way, where have you been?'

Before she could reply Jolyon answered for her. 'We've been to buy a Christmas tree from Mr Bradshaw's farm, and when it comes we're going to put little lights on it, aren't we, Polly?'

'Yes,' she cried excitedly, 'and Father Christmas is coming soon. Will he be bringing presents for you, Dr Hamilton?'

He smiled. 'I'm not sure. And, Polly, my name is Glenn. Do you think I should send him a letter?'

Two small fair heads nodded simultaneously and Polly said, 'If he doesn't bring you any, you can come and play with our toys, can't he, Jolly?'

'Yes, you can,' he agreed solemnly.

'I will remember that,' he told them with the same degree of seriousness, and turned to Anna, who was keeping a low profile. 'Is it a large tree?'

'Yes,' she replied, not sure to be glad or sorry at his cool dismissal of the previous night's happenings.

'Right, so when it's delivered let me know if you have any trouble moving it to where you want it to stand. OK?'

'Yes,' she agreed weakly, and thought it would have to be really heavy for her to do that in the light of recent events.

# CHAPTER SIX

IT *WAS* heavy. Bill brought the tree into the house for her and propped it up in the corner where she wanted it to stand, but she couldn't lift it into the big bronze pot that was always brought down from the attic on such occasions, and as the children were eager to begin decorating it, Anna ended up going to find Glenn.

She found him occupied in taking the black bag out of the waste bin in the kitchen, and right on top of the rubbish was the food from the night before. 'So you didn't eat it after all,' she said regretfully. 'What *did* you have?'

'Nothing,' he replied, and as she groaned he went on to say, 'Another minute and I'd have had the bag tied up. But does it matter?'

'No. I suppose not,' she conceded hastily. 'I've come about your offer to help with the tree. I could have waited until James gets back but the children are bursting for us to start decorating it and it might be past their bedtime when he arrives.'

'Sure,' he said easily. 'I'll wash my hands and be with you in a couple of seconds.' And on that assurance she left him to follow.

'That is some big tree,' he said, when he'd positioned it in the pot and surrounded it with stones from the garden to keep it upright. He turned to Polly and Jolly, who were dancing around him excitedly. 'What I want to know is who is going to put the fairy on the top. Do you know any giants?'

They shook their heads, solemn for a moment, and then, realising that he was teasing, Polly squealed, 'You can do it!'

'All right, then,' he agreed. Opening out the stepladder that Anna had got in readiness, he picked up the little tinsel fairy and climbed up with her in his hand. When he was high enough Glenn looked down at Anna's upturned face and said, 'I wasn't intending to muscle in on the tree-decorating. I'll make myself scarce once I've fixed the fairy.'

'You don't have to,' she said in a low voice. 'This is different from last night. It's just family stuff.'

'And what was last night?'

'A moment of madness. I should have had more sense.'

'Maybe we both should, but do we have to feel guilty over something that was innocent and above-board?'

'The fairy, the fairy!' the children were shouting, and remembering what he was up there for he reached over and placed her firmly where she could look down at them all.

'You didn't answer my question,' he said when he was back at floor level.

'It shouldn't have happened,' she said, keeping her voice low so the children couldn't hear. 'Let's drop the subject and concentrate on decorating the tree.'

He stared at her for a moment, then slowly nodded

and began to fold up the ladder. 'Well, I promised not to linger so I'll let you get on.'

She looked at him and sighed. 'Glenn, let's not spoil this. Why don't you stay and help us?'

'I'd be pleased to, but are you suggesting it because you're thinking that there's safety in numbers, by any chance?'

'No, not at all,' she said coolly. 'It's a big tree and some of the branches are quite high up.'

He smiled and the tension broke. As they hung ornaments on the branches she said, 'Some of these glass baubles are old. They were on the tree when James and I were small, and the rest are the usual plastic. Unbreakable but lacking the same delicacy.'

It was a happy time, and Anna loved watching Glenn help the children carefully hang the decorations. Polly and Jolly were entranced as the bareness of the spruce gradually disappeared beneath the ornaments, tinsel and fairy-lights.

When the last bauble had been hung and the last piece of tinsel draped across the fresh green branches, he said, 'What about your tree, Anna? Did you ask the farmer to deliver a tree for you at the same time? By the way, I still haven't been invited to your place. You haven't got a guilty secret to hide, have you?'

The joking comment hit a nerve, even though it had been made in all innocence. He saw her flinch and wondered why.

But she managed another smile and told him, 'I've hardly been in my own home since you arrived, but I'll be going back once James is with us again, so feel free to call if you want. As for the tree, I have a small artificial one that I bring out each year. Maybe not the most atmospheric of things but it looks all right once I've decorated it, which is usually at the last minute on Christmas Eve. It has one snag, though. I miss the lovely woodland smell that a real spruce brings with it.'

When James arrived home the children were waiting for him on the doorstep dressed in pyjamas and dressing-gowns, and as he came up the path they called to him to close his eyes. He obeyed and they led him inside in high glee to where the tree stood in the sitting room, lights twinkling.

'Now you can open them, Daddy,' they cried, and as Anna and Glenn looked on smilingly he did as he was told and expressed his delight and amazement.

'How on earth did you manage to get such a large tree in position?' he said when Glenn had tactfully left the four of them together and gone up to his room.

'Bill Bradshaw delivered it as usual and Glenn lifted it into the pot.'

'You must have been glad to have him around. I do hope he's going to enjoy Christmas in Willowmere.'

'He says he's looking forward to joining us as he hasn't had much experience of a family Christmas, but he doesn't want to be in the way.'

'What did you say to that?'

'I assured him that he wouldn't be.'

'And I'm sure that you meant it. Though you've never said how you feel about him. Are you in love with the guy, Anna?'

It was not a moment for the truth, she decided but James was waiting for an answer, so avoiding the issues that being honest would bring she said lightly, 'The only male who pulls at my heart strings is there in his pyjamas, and I think it's time he and his sister were tucked up for the night. Do you want to do the bedtime-story bit, or shall I? It's been a long day for you.'

'Not so long that I would want to miss my time with the children,' he replied, and with a smile for her added, 'Anna, just for the record, I can tell when I'm being side-tracked.'

She returned to the annexe later in the evening, just as she'd told Glenn she would, and as her small but tasteful home welcomed her back into quietness she wondered when he would come, but Sunday passed and he didn't appear.

When she arrived at the surgery on Monday morning, after seeing the children safely to school, it was already a hive of activity, with stragglers who'd left it rather late for their flu jabs waiting outside the nurses' rooms in company with those who'd come for the usual blood tests and so on.

She'd seen Glenn briefly at breakfast-time. He and James had been about to go to the surgery as she'd arrived to get the children dressed and ready for school, and they'd just exchanged brief greetings. Now that she was here, there was no sign of him. The door to his consulting room was shut, indicating that he was with a patient, and at that moment Bill Bradshaw came out, looking rather red-faced.

When he saw her he said, 'I did what you told me to do, made an appointment to see one of the doctors, and he's sendin' me fer tests.'

She nodded approvingly. 'Good thinking. I'm sure that Betty must have thought so.'

'Aye, she did. The wife has been on at me for weeks to do something about it, and talkin' to you when you came for the tree spurred me on.'

He jerked his thumb towards the room he'd just left. 'Seems to know what he's on about, yon fellow, even though he is a southerner.'

'Get away with you,' she said laughingly. 'A lot of the top-rankers of the medical profession are based in the southern counties.'

'Really? Well, it's fellows like your father that I prefer to see. The old-style country doctor kind, if you get what I mean.'

'James, Georgina *and* Glenn are all excellent doctors,' she protested mildly.

'Maybe, but I reckon they wouldn't recognise a bottle of castor oil if it jumped up and bit 'em.'

She was laughing again. 'Maybe not, and thanks be for that!' And with her glance on those waiting to see a nurse, she left him to amble off with his home-spun philosophies.

Young Josh was one of those waiting to be seen and she was pleased to see that the infection had cleared and the sore spot had healed.

'Do you know that my mother is going to have a baby, Anna?' he asked when he was ready to go.

'Yes, I do,' she told him. 'How do you feel about it, Josh?'

'It's great, just as long as I don't have to push it out in the buggy in front of my mates. I hope it's a boy.'

'A little sister would be just as nice.'

'Like Polly, you mean?'

'Yes, maybe. Now, mind how you go. No more messing about with rusty nails.'

'He's a nice kid, that one,' Beth said when he'd gone. 'Let's hope he's as thrilled when the house is full of baby things and junior is teething.'

There was still no sign of Glenn. She could hear his door opening and shutting down the passage as patients came and went, but he hadn't yet ventured forth for any reason. Eventually one of the receptionists came round with elevenses and then he appeared, mug in hand.

'Hello, there,' he said, framed in the doorway and addressing them both, but with his glance on Anna. 'Everything all right?'

'Yes,' Beth said breezily. 'It's a typical Monday morning, with the regulars and those who've fallen by the wayside over the weekend.'

Anna's expression was sombre. It had only been a short time since she'd gone back into her own place, leaving Glenn at Bracken House, yet it seemed much longer. How she would cope if he didn't settle in Willowmere, she shuddered to think. Yet common sense said that would be the best thing in the long run.

'Was it good to be back where you belong?' he asked as Beth was bringing up their last patient's records on the computer and labelling the blood sample she'd just taken.

'Mmm, it was nice. I slept with an easy mind, knowing that James was back, Jolyon was much better and you were next door, too.'

'Good,' he said without further comment, and went back into his room.

* * *

It was a cold night. A winter moon hung over the village and as lights in the windows and gardens of the cottages twinkled out to where the trees stood fronded with frost, the magic of Christmas was taking hold of Willowmere.

It was not surprising that Anna loved this place, Glenn was thinking as he looked out across the village green from his bedroom window. It was wooing him, enchanting him with its peace and timelessness. There was no sound of gunfire to make him flinch, or the never-ending grind of the traffic of a big city, just the quiet of the countryside.

Yet he hadn't given up the idea of going back to the kind of work he'd been doing before the longing to see Anna again had become unbearable and he'd flown home. But if he ever went abroad again he would want her with him, in his bed at night whenever the chance to sleep presented itself and by his side in the daytime. He'd come back to find some normality and she was it. Together, as husband and wife, doctor and nurse, they could accomplish much.

But there was the small matter of getting her to see his point of view and it wasn't going to be easy or soon. If he kept harassing her, it wouldn't be fair. He had no right to interfere in her life to such an extent. She had set herself on a course that she felt she must keep to, and he loved her for it.

He would have liked to tell James how he felt about Anna but it would be putting the onus on him and he, Glenn, had no way of knowing what kind of disruption it would cause, as he didn't know if Anna had ever told her brother just how deeply they had once been involved...

It was clear that the two of them, James and Anna,

had a loving bond and that his arrival back in her life had not at first been as welcome as the flowers in spring as far as she was concerned, yet once he'd discovered that she was still single he'd begun to hope.

If she could convince him that she didn't want him enough to change her lifestyle, he would go back to where he'd come from—but he would have to be sure, and if the way she'd responded to him the other night was anything to go by, she wanted him just as much as he wanted her.

He pulled a warm jacket out of the wardrobe and went out into the frosty night. When he knocked on Anna's door there was no answer and the lights weren't on so, surmising that she might be at the village hall, he walked in that direction, but that too was in darkness.

Now that he'd ventured out, he was reluctant to go back inside so soon and pointed himself in the direction of the lake, deciding that if he couldn't be with Anna he could at least spend a few moments at the place she held so dear.

He wondered if it ever froze over enough for the locals to skate on. That would be a sight to behold, but there were no signs of anything like that when he got there, just a solitary car parked by the lakeside with its headlights shining across its still waters. He smiled. It would be lovers, wanting to be unobserved, he'd like to bet.

That was until he saw the make of the car and its number plate. His eyes widened. It was Anna's car, and even as it registered he was hoping that she'd got the doors securely locked.

When he tapped on the window on the driver's side,

she was sitting staring into space, but she turned her head at the sound and when she saw him it was her turn to be surprised.

'Glenn! What are *you* doing here?' she exclaimed, getting out of the car to stand beside him.

'I should be asking you that,' he said evenly. 'I was expecting it to be a courting couple in the car and was about to give it a wide berth until I saw the number plate.'

'I came out here to think. James was going over the practice accounts, the children were tucked up for the night, and for once I didn't have a pile of ironing staring me in the face. And, as I've already explained, this is my favourite part of the village.'

'Yes, I'm aware of that,' he told her, and thought of the watercolour painted by Alex Graham that he'd bought from the gallery as a Christmas gift for her.

The event that brought joy to every dark winter would soon be here, and he had a feeling that he shouldn't have accepted her invitation to share it with them, that he would be butting in on a family occasion, Yet he'd agreed to join them and that was it, and if he didn't get any closer to Anna over Christmas, he would just have to suffer in silence.

'Does the lake ever freeze over?' he asked as they stood looking at the moon reflected in its waters.

'Yes, sometimes, and then we all turn up with our skates, but it has to be well below zero for that to happen.'

'I could stay here for ever,' he said softly. 'It's beautiful in moonlight on a frosty night, Anna, and so are you.' She turned to look at him and for a moment he saw the desire he felt reflected in her eyes, and he ached to draw her into his arms.

'Please, don't, Glenn,' she whispered. 'I can't give you what you want. If you want to put roots down in Willowmere, then stay, but it's for you to decide. You know the score.'

She was moving towards the car. The spell had been broken. 'Do you want to walk back, or can I give you a lift?' she asked, not meeting his gaze.

'I'll walk, thanks,' he informed her flatly, 'though I'm not going until I've seen you safely on your way.'

'All right, whatever you say,' she said in a similar tone to his, and when the engine spluttered into life she waved briefly and he watched her drive off into the night.

When Anna arrived home she went slowly upstairs, thinking as she did so that it had been perfect by the lake, just the two of them in the quiet night. When she'd realised what had been about to happen between them she'd had to stop it, though it had nearly broken her heart. But at least she had finally told him something of the truth. That she couldn't give him what she knew he wanted.

Still in a melancholy mood she walked across to the window and looked out over the village, as Glenn had done earlier, and saw him returning, but instead of going into Bracken House he went to the boot of his car and as he reached inside she turned away. Whatever he was doing, it wasn't her concern, she decided, but as she was taking her jacket off the doorbell rang and her heartbeat quickened. What now? she thought.

When she opened the door he was holding a tree, half

the size of the one they'd decorated previously but just as fresh and sweet smelling, and as she eyed him in surprise he reached out and placed it just inside the hallway.

'Peace offering,' he said, and smiled.

'Oh, Glenn,' she breathed, returning his smile and wishing so much for their situation to be different. 'Please, won't you come in?'

He shook his head. 'No, not now. It's late. But I'll come and help you decorate it tomorrow night, if you like, now that I've honed my Christmas-tree decorating skills.'

She was laughing, gloomy thoughts put to one side, and he thought how lovely she was as she breathed in the Christmassy scent of the small but perfect tree.

'That would be great,' she said. 'And thanks for the lovely surprise.'

'My pleasure,' he replied and went.


The next morning at the surgery Beth said, 'We've heard from our Jess, Anna. She'll be home soon. She's passed the course for nursery nursing or becoming a nanny, so now it's going to be job-hunting.'

'I can't see her having much trouble there,' Anna commented. She liked Beth's capable and cheerful daughter immensely. 'She's a natural with children. The twins love it when she calls round.'

'Jess has certainly chosen the right vocation,' Beth agreed, 'but I hope she doesn't end up in America or somewhere else far away. Her dad and I would be desolate without her, and deep down Jess is really a home bird.'

The chairs outside in the corridor were filling up and

as the morning progressed they were too busy to think of anything but the patients, for which Anna was thankful.

But in rare quiet moments the events of the previous night occupied her mind. They'd been spellbound by the glittering beauty of Willowmere in moonlight and it would have been so easy to have gone one step further. But doing so would only have brought more heartache, and she was determined that tonight, when he came round to help her decorate the tree, nothing would happen between them.

Glenn's door remained closed and in the middle of the morning James informed her that he had gone out on an urgent call before she'd arrived and was still not back.

'What was the problem?' she asked.

'The gypsies have arrived for their yearly visit to these parts and have camped at their usual site for a while,' he explained. 'As you are aware, in recent years they've registered with us because of the length of their stay, hence the request for a visit. It sounded as if one of their members is quite poorly.

'I'm not sure if any of them have had the flu vacci-nation as that was what it sounded like—a bad case of flu or maybe pneumonia. Glenn rang in a few moments ago to say that half of them are unwell. He's been checking out more than the one patient and is waiting for public health to arrive as there seems to be a stomach bug also doing the rounds amongst them.'

'Oh, dear!' she exclaimed. 'We've known them for years and they've never had anything too serious while they've been here. I hope it doesn't get worse.'

'So do I,' he agreed. 'However, this time it might be

different if it is some sort of gastric bug that isn't nipped in the bud. But Glenn has got it all under control. Infection will never have been far away in the places he's been working in. I hope he is with us for a long time to come and have a feeling that how long he stays will depend on you.'

'It will be up to him, not me. He knows where I stand,' she told him, but knew she didn't sound very convincing.

James didn't pursue it. Instead, he informed her, 'He's sending those who are still standing for the flu jab so you and Beth have a busy time ahead once they arrive.'

She smiled. 'I'd better be getting on, then.'

When Glenn returned, the gypsies had been for their vaccinations and gone. He reported that the patient he'd been called out to had been taken to hospital with suspected pneumonia, and that he'd given out prescriptions to those with the stomach upsets and left them in the care of public health.

'Who was it that you had admitted to hospital?' asked Anna.

He looked at her in surprise. 'Why? Do you know them personally?'

'I know some of them, yes. We usually expect the gypsies at this time of year. They've come as long as I can remember and the villagers have no problem with them. They keep themselves to themselves and don't leave a mess when they go.'

'It was an older guy called Marco who has got pneumonia.'

'I know him. He's usually in charge. Was Montrose there?'

'How would I know?'

'Monty is Marco's son and devoted to his parents.'

'There was a tall, dark-haired fellow hovering all the time I was doing the rounds.'

She nodded. 'That would probably be him and it explains why he didn't come for the flu jab like the others. He would have gone to the hospital with his father. Monty is a friend of mine. We played together when we were kids and enjoy meeting up each year for a short time.'

Anna spending a *short* time with Monty suited *him* fine, Glenn thought. The fellow had been attractive in a flashy sort of way, but they couldn't be that close or Anna would have known the gypsies had arrived and she hadn't been aware of it until he'd rung in to report on what he'd found when he'd got there.

It was a quarter to three and Anna was about to go and meet the children from school when Monty came strolling into the surgery at the same moment that Glenn arrived back from the rest of his delayed house calls.

'How are you, Anna?' he said with a smile. 'The new doctor has been very good to us. Has he told you about my father?'

'Yes,' she said gently. 'How is Marco now?'

His smile faded. 'Not good. They say at the hospital it is pneumonia. My mother is with him while I go back to see to the others who are sick.'

As Glenn went into the surgery kitchen to prepare a belated lunch he heard Monty say, 'There is something I wanted to ask you, Anna. I hope you'll say yes.'

ABIGAIL GORDON 113

He didn't hear the rest. They'd moved down the
passage out of earshot and he had a sinking feeling that
he wouldn't want to hear, even if he could. Her face
didn't light up like that when *he* put in an appearance.
When he came out of the kitchen with a sandwich in one
hand and a mug of tea in the other, Monty had gone.
Anna was about to leave, and she was still smiling.

'It is obvious that someone's face fits,' he said whimsically. 'I'll have to ask him what his secret is.'

The smile wavered. 'I don't know what you're talking
about,' she said, 'but tell me something—are you into
weddings?'

Glenn froze and said stiffly, 'It all depends on who
is getting married.'

'I'm talking about a gypsy wedding. Monty has invited
us to his wedding to Tabitha, the daughter of one of the
families that travel with them. He has asked me because
I'm a friend from his childhood, and you're invited
because of the way you've looked after his people today.'

He relaxed. 'When is it to be?' he questioned in an
upbeat tone that made her glance at him in surprise.

'Next week, if his father is well enough to be there.'
She looked at him and frowned. 'Glenn! Are you crazy?
Surely you didn't think I was going to be the bride? He's
just a friend from way back. We don't see each other
from one year to the next. So, are you going to take me
to his wedding or not?'

'Yes, of course. I can't think of anything I would
like more.'

Glenn walked back to his room with a lighter step.
That wasn't strictly true, of course. There were lots of
things they could do together that would outclass going

to Monty's wedding, such as making love and planning a future. But it was a start.

That evening, James had just taken the children upstairs to spend time with them before putting them to bed. Anna was tidying up after the meal when Glenn said, 'What about a wedding gift for Monty? Are we going to join or buy separate presents? There's only the coming Saturday for us to go shopping, or maybe we could take advantage of the late-night Christmas hours during the week. What do you think?'

'I think we should give them a joint gift, and late-night shopping won't be as crowded as a Saturday so near Christmas.'

'I agree,' he said. 'How about tomorrow night? And have you any suggestions? For instance, does Monty have his own caravan?'

Anna shook her head. 'No. A gypsy couple don't move into their own home until the first child is born. Before that the bride lives with her in-laws and helps generally on the domestic front. Their customs are very different to ours. Often the marriage ceremony is just a matter of the bride and groom holding hands in front of everyone and promising to be true to each other.

'Marriages amongst them could almost be classed as arranged. The father of the bridegroom pays a sum of money, what we would call a dowry, to the bride's father to recompense him for the loss of his daughter, and it is the parents who make the wedding arrangements.'

'You seem to be well informed,' he commented.

'I am. I've never had an invitation before, but I've watched a few of their weddings from a distance, and I think I should warn you that the festivities go on for days.'

He smiled. 'Not for us, I hope!'

'No, of course not. I think our patients would have something to say if we were missing for that length of time.' Anna's eyes twinkled. 'We'll just have to make our excuses when we're ready to go.'

'And so getting back to the wedding gift?' he prompted.

'I don't know. I'll give it some thought. Their own people usually give them money so that when the first-born comes along and they move into their own caravan, they have some savings to fall back on, but as outsiders I feel it might seem intrusive if we do that.'

'So tomorrow night it is,' he confirmed, and when she didn't reply immediately he went on, 'Are you sure? We'll have been in each other's company at the surgery during the day, and will be together all the time we're shopping. I wouldn't want you to feel you are having an overdose of my company, as I haven't forgotten our arrangement for tonight with regard to a certain tree.'

I could never have too much of your company, she thought, even though we seem to move from one delicate situation to the next. I've been starved of it for years.

'I'll risk it,' she replied lightly.

'Be it upon your own head,' he said whimsically, and then went on to say, 'What time do you want me round to help fix the tree?''

'When I've cleared away here,' she told him, and hoped that the rest of the evening would be amicable and stress-free.

\* \* \*

To Anna's relief it was. There was no dressing up on her part tonight. When she opened the door to Glenn she was wearing the inevitable jeans with a cotton top, scant make-up and minus perfume, and he had to hide a smile.

The message was loud and clear and it would have been easy to tell her that she was beautiful to him no matter what, but he'd already decided that tonight there was going to be nothing but friendliness as they decorated the tree that he'd brought her, and that was how it was as they hung less fragile baubles than those on the tree next door and put a star on top instead of a fairy.

When it was done Anna smiled her satisfaction and told him, 'My tree had never been in place so early or looked so good, and it is thanks to you.'

The Christmas spirit was taking hold of them, he thought, and said laughingly, 'So shall I take a bow or put the kettle on?'

'Both,' she replied, matching his mood, and while he was in the kitchen she switched on a CD of carols and left them playing softly in the background.

They sat in silence by the fire, drinking the coffee she'd made and listening to the music. She wished it could go on for ever, with no questions to answer, no anxieties regarding those she loved, and as if he'd read her mind Glenn said, 'Sometimes I think we fret too much for the things we can't have and miss out on what is already there.'

Anna didn't reply because tears were threatening and she didn't want to break the peace between them in these quiet moments, but it didn't stop her from wondering if, unknown to him, his words had held a message for her. But it wasn't as simple as that...was it?

He went not long after and she didn't try to stop him. His departing words had a comfort all of their own. 'Goodnight, Anna. I'll see you tomorrow.' She rejoiced at the thought.

# CHAPTER SEVEN

'ENJOY your shopping trip,' James said the next evening as Anna and Glenn prepared to go out to buy a wedding gift for Montrose and Tabitha. 'Have you warned Glenn that their weddings are not short affairs?'

'Yes, I have been warned,' Glenn said as he came downstairs, ready to leave.

Anna was laughing and he thought how great it was to see her happy as she said, 'Maybe I should also explain that huge sides of beef and pork will be roasting above the fire for hours before the ceremony begins and, as I've already said, it could go on for ever.'

'So there'll be lots of gravy,' he joked, and her eyes sparkled back at him.

'I can see that you two are going to enjoy every minute of this wedding,' James said, and would have liked to have followed it with, *When are you going to do something about a wedding of your own?* But there was no way he would want to embarrass them, although when the moment was right he intended to have a serious talk with his sister.

* * *

As they strolled from store to store Glenn took Anna's hand in his and she let it stay in his warm clasp. It was all around them, the excitement and expectancy of Christmas and as they stopped beside Santa seated in front of a huge tree in one of the shopping malls he said, 'I can't believe that we're going to be together for one of the happiest times of the year.'

He was smiling, but when she looked up at him he sensed that the habitual wariness in her that was like a barrier between them was back.

'What?' he asked. 'Don't you feel the same, Anna?'

'Yes,' she replied, and thought that Glenn wasn't the only one who'd had some lonely Christmastimes. It was possible to be with relatives and friends, surrounded by affection and goodwill, and yet still feel alone.

'Has James ever thought of remarrying?' he asked with an easiness that concealed the importance of the question as they watched children taking their turn to sit on Santa's knee.

'I don't know. Maybe. We haven't discussed it, but I wouldn't want him to rush into any decision that he might regret on my account,' she said levelly. 'He adored Julie and she was like a sister to me so, you see, I don't look upon the life I lead as a penance.'

'I never thought you did, but don't you want children of your own one day? I'm sure James would wish that for you.'

James wouldn't want for me what I can't have, she thought despondently. It was another opportunity to be honest with Glenn, to tell him that circumstance had denied her children, but once again the words stuck in her throat, and instead of giving him a direct answer, she sidetracked his comment by saying, 'I have Pollyanna and Jolyon in my life. They're all I need.'

He wasn't prepared to leave it at that. 'Yes, but—'

'Can't we talk about something else?' she interrupted flatly.

'Sure,' he agreed with the same deceptive easiness, and pointed to a shop that sold kitchenware.

They chose a huge casserole dish from a well-known brand as a gift for Montrose and Tabitha. It would hold enough to feed both their families and more besides, and having felt the weight of it they arranged for the store to deliver it the next day.

When that was accomplished and Anna had bought a few extras to go in the children's stockings he said, 'Shall we go for a coffee? Or find a bar somewhere?'

He'd stopped holding her hand after what had ended up as a depressing insight into her mind and now just wanted them to sit quietly in some place where they could unwind and talk about ordinary everyday things rather than the rest of their lives, which always ended up in heartache.

'A glass of wine would be nice if we can find somewhere that isn't crowded,' she replied, feeling remorseful after bringing gloom into the precious time they were spending together. 'There's a bar near where we parked the car, but it won't be much fun for you if you're driving.'

'An orange juice will suit me fine,' he said, 'so let's go and see if we can get a couple of seats.'

The place was crowded and it was noisy, but the atmosphere was good as everyone seemed happy enough to be out and about on a night so near Christmas.

They managed to find a small table tucked away next to a large Christmas tree, and Glenn went to the bar, returning with a glass of wine for Anna and an orange juice for himself. Settling into his chair, he said, 'So, tell me what Pollyanna and Jolyon are getting for Christmas and bring me up to date with what is going to be happening in the village during the next two weeks.'

Relieved to be on safe ground again, she smiled. 'Santa is bringing Polly a new doll and a buggy to push her out in, plus a pretty party frock and some ballet shoes as she's going to start having lessons after Christmas.

'Jolyon has asked Santa for a fort and a fireman's outfit, and they're both getting their first little bikes, so there'll be some excitement on Christmas morning. If you feel like getting up at the crack of dawn you'll be on the spot to watch them as they discover what has arrived while they've been asleep.'

'I'd like that,' he said, and immediately wondered what he could buy for the children that they hadn't already got.

She was smiling across at him and it wiped away any pain that their previous conversation might have caused as she said, 'And as to what will be happening in Willowmere, the answer is lots of things. There's the Mistletoe Ball that I told you about on the Saturday before Christmas Day, and this year it has been decided to hold it in a huge marquee on the school playing fields.

'The candlelit carol service in the church is on the Sunday after the ball, followed by coffee and mince pies at the vicarage, and then some of us go round the village to sing for the people who couldn't get to the service.'

'What do you do for music?'

'We have our own brass band to accompany us.'

'Really? I wouldn't mind being involved in that if I had my trumpet. It got left behind in the last-minute rush to get to the airport when I was coming home and I don't expect to see it again, but even so I will enjoy hearing them play.'

She was pleased to see his interest and told him, 'I thought you'd be impressed to know we have our own band.'

'I most certainly am,' he affirmed, and she recalled how he'd loved playing the trumpet at every opportunity and how talented he'd been. She'd been debating what to give him as a Christmas gift and knew now that nothing would please him more than a new instrument to replace the one he'd lost.

Glenn's thoughts were running along different channels. 'So how do I get us tickets for the ball?' he was asking.

'Jack and Amy at the post office are selling them and will have kept some for James and me. It's a very popular occasion, gives everyone a chance to dress up, which brings us back to the matter of your dinner jacket and dress shirt.'

'And the bow-tie that goes with it.'

'Yes.'

'No problem. If we'd thought of it earlier I could have got kitted out tonight. What time is the wedding on Saturday?'

'Four in the afternoon.'

'So I'll come into town first thing in the morning and get my outfit for the ball sorted. Do you and James attend as a regular thing?'

'No. It isn't always convenient.'

'Don't you ever leave the children with a child-minder?'

'Yes, occasionally, but there's only one person we trust to look after them and she hasn't been available of late.'

'Who is she, some teenager who needs the cash?'

'Not exactly, Jess is twenty-two and the daughter of Beth, the other nurse at the surgery. She's a lovely girl and dotes on Polly and Jolly. We haven't seen much of her in recent weeks as she's been on a course, but she'll be coming to see us some time soon.'

As they drove home Glenn said, 'So I'll have a word with your friends at the post office regarding tickets. Will they have put three to one side by any chance? If there are only two, I can't take James's.'

'Don't worry. I'll ask him if he intends going, but I doubt it. He'll be pleased to hear that I'm going, but will almost certainly say no with regard to joining us. His evenings are taken up with practice work and getting ready for Santa's visit.'

When Glenn stopped the car in front of the surgery she already had her door key in her hand and was out in a flash. Getting the message, he said softly, 'Goodnight, Anna,' and stayed on his side of the car to avoid throwing all his promises to the wind and sweeping her into his arms.

'No, thanks just the same,' James said when Anna asked him if he wanted to go to the ball. 'For one thing, Jess isn't around to ask if she will mind the children, but I'm pleased that Glenn is taking you.'

He'd had a few enquiries from available women of the village as to whether he would be present on the occasion and had known they'd been fishing for invitations, but he was aware that if he appeared in front of everyone with someone local it would set tongues wagging, and he had no taste for that. If he ever found someone to replace Julie he would be happy for the whole world to know, but that day had yet to come.

In the middle of the following morning Clare Halliday, the elegant, middle-aged owner of the art gallery, came to the nurses' room to have blood tests taken at Georgina's request.

'I've just seen Dr Adams, Anna,' she said worriedly, 'and I've a feeling that she thinks I might have something wrong with me. She wants to see me again as soon as the results of the tests come back.'

'So what might make her think that, Clare?' Anna asked. 'It isn't often we see you at the surgery.'

'Yes, I know,' she replied. 'I'm here because I've had heartburn and indigestion for months and nothing I take seems to relieve it. Also my stomach is sticking out a mile. I look as if I'm six months pregnant, and to make matters worse my mother has come to live with me and she is not the easiest of people to get on with. I've also got the business to run, which is what I enjoy doing the most.' She sighed. 'Talking about the business, the new doctor was in the other day, buying a watercolour by a local artist. He's very attractive.'

'Yes, that would be Dr Hamilton,' Anna told her, and

thought that the description suited the man who was half in and half out of her life very well.

When she'd taken the blood she told Clare, 'Dr Adams has asked for a quick report on these tests so you should know something soon.' And added with a comforting smile, 'So go home and try not to worry until the results come through. It could be something quite simple that is causing the symptoms.'

'I hope so,' she said dismally as she prepared to depart. 'One hears of such dreadful things these days.'

The owner of the picture gallery had barely closed the outer door of the surgery behind her before Georgina appeared in the nurses' room.

'Has Clare Halliday had the bloods taken?' she asked, and when Anna pointed to the phials ready for off she said, 'I'm very concerned about her.' And on that sober comment she went back down the corridor to where the rest of her patients were waiting.

'What do you think she meant?' Beth said when she'd gone.

'Who knows?' Anna said. 'But Georgina doesn't let the grass grow under her feet. If the results show anything that could be serious she'll send Clare to see a specialist without delay.'

Saturday mornings were not as hectic as weekdays. There wasn't the same urgency to get the children ready and off to school, and as Anna stood gazing out at a frosty morning from the window of her sitting room she saw Glenn striding purposefully down the path towards his car.

Her heartbeat quickened as it always did at the sight

of him. He was tall, dark-haired, dark-eyed and lean, every woman's dream man. Yet it was still her that he seemed to want, the nondescript practice nurse with hazel eyes set in a plain face, her only claim to beauty being her red-gold hair. What *did* he see in her?

He must have decided to go into town early to get the suit before the place became packed with Christmas shoppers, and as he drove off without being aware of her at the window Anna's mind was on the days to come.

Days when the life she'd made with James and the children would still go on. Not because it had to, James would never tie her down with his domestic problems if she wanted to stretch her wings. It would be because she had nowhere else to go.

Having Glenn in Willowmere was a mixture of joy and sadness to her. Every moment they spent together was engraved upon her heart, and if he should tire of her lack of response and decide to go away again, the memory of those times during one of the most special seasons of the year would have to suffice.

Like the wedding they were going to in just a few hours, where Montrose and Tabitha would make their vows to each other in front of their families and the others who travelled with them. There would be no trappings of church or registry office, just two people in the dusk of a December afternoon promising to be faithful.

Once that was done the festivities would start, the food and the wine, an abundance of it, with music all around them. And when their appetites were appeased there would be dancing around the campfire and lots of good-natured merriment.

When Glenn's car had disappeared from sight she went upstairs to get out the clothes she intended to wear. They consisted of a brightly coloured shawl of greens and gold that suited her colouring perfectly, and a warm top to go underneath to keep out the cold. Matching the shawl was a long green skirt, flared so that it would swirl around her as she danced. Calf-high boots on her feet completed the outfit.

As she took in the effect, excitement was rising inside her. She'd felt threatened ever since Glenn had come back into her life. He'd shattered the safe cocoon that had gradually formed around her as she'd accepted what the fates had meted out on an icy road five years ago.

But today it was different. She felt alive, ready to throw off her cares for a while. Remembering how he had accepted her stipulation of no strings attached, what could possibly go wrong?

He rang her bell in the late morning and informed her that he'd bought a suit for the ball and gifts for the children, who hadn't yet got back from their Saturday morning visit to the park with James.

He'd brought the presents with him and said, 'I thought you could whisk them out of sight while Pollyanna and Jolyon aren't around.'

'Yes, and thanks for remembering them,' she said softly, and wondered if he was thinking that it might be the nearest he was ever going to get to being with children in a family setting at Christmas. Unless he gave up on her and chose someone else to give him little ones. The thought was like a knife in her heart.

'Do you want to come in?' she asked, stepping back, but he shook his head.

'Another time maybe. I'm going to clean the car and then have a shower. Are we walking or driving to the wedding? The gypsy camp isn't that far, is it, but it is cold out here.'

'Let's walk,' she said, eyes bright with anticipation, and he observed her with raised brows but didn't comment.

'Yes, all right,' he agreed. 'But are we sure it's on for today? What about the old guy I had admitted to hospital? Didn't you say that he's the bridegroom's father?'

'Yes, and I've checked that he's home, but Marco will have to watch the proceedings from inside the caravan and keep warm.'

'And how are we going to keep warm? What are you intending wearing?'

'A shawl, a long skirt and boots, with gold hoops in my ears. What about you?'

'I'm not sure. Probably a shirt and black trousers, with boots and a leather jacket. What do you think?'

'That sounds fine to be wearing as we mingle with them, though I'm expecting the folks there to be decked out in their finery. I saw an advert for wedding dresses for gypsy brides once and some of them were very impressive, heavily beaded in Renaissance styles, so we'll have to wait and see. It's not far to the site so if you call for me at a quarter past three it should be soon enough.'

'Are you looking forward to it?' he asked.

'Yes, of course I am.'

'Although I'm the one who is taking you?'

*Was he kidding?* 'That's one of the reasons why.'

'Really! So I'd better not let you down, had I?' he

commented dryly, and her smile faltered, but she didn't take him up on it, just said goodbye as he turned to go and went to hide the gifts he'd brought.

'I hope that the casserole dish was delivered safely,' Glenn said as they walked towards the gypsy camp in the winter dusk, and when Anna nodded without speaking he said, 'So what's wrong? Has the bubble burst? You were up in the clouds this morning.'

She managed a smile and even managed to sound convincing as she said, 'I'm fine. I was just thinking that I won't be moving far from the fire. There is frost on the trees already. It's going to be a cold night.'

In truth, she wasn't thinking anything of the sort. It was something that Polly had said in all innocence when they'd called after they'd been to the park that had hit her where it hurt the most. Her small niece had been listening to the two adults discussing the wedding and had said, 'What's a bride, Anna?'

'It is a beautiful lady in a long white dress,' she'd told her, 'who is marrying a man like your daddy because she loves him.'

'Was Mummy a beautiful bride?'

'Yes, she was,' James had told her gently.

'When are you going to be a bride, Anna?' had been her next question.

'When I find someone as nice as your daddy?' she'd said lightly.

But when she'd met James's glance it had been grave and he'd said quietly, 'From out of the mouths of babes, Anna.'

That had been upsetting enough but Polly still hadn't

finished. She'd had one more thing to say and it had been a corker. 'Can't you be Dr Glenn's bride, Anna? He hasn't got anybody to love him.'

'I think I hear Jolyon calling you, Polly,' James had said hurriedly.

Quite unaware that she'd just hit the nail on the head, the little girl had skipped off to see what her brother was up to, and when she'd gone Anna had said tonelessly, 'If only it was that simple, James. Glenn wants a family and I can't give him one.'

'So you haven't told him?'

'No. I can't force him into a corner where he has to choose between me and having children.'

'He might just wish you had if he ever finds out,' he'd warned. 'You're not being exactly fair to him.'

She'd had nothing to say to that and had just shaken her head dejectedly. Of course, Polly had spoken in childish innocence. Of course, James wanted only what was best for her, she'd told herself as she'd changed into her clothes for the wedding, but why did she feel as if she was being badgered from all sides by those she loved? She was quite capable of sorting out her own life…or was she?

And now Glenn, who didn't miss a thing where she was concerned, was tuning into her low spirits, asking what was wrong. Not wanting him to think it was anything he'd done, she'd used the weather as a trite reason for being low key compared to how she'd been that morning.

The warm welcome they received from the wedding party when they joined them wiped away the blues and

Anna found her mood lightening with every second as they stood beside a large bonfire and smelt the succulence of roasting meat.

Glenn was close beside her and every time she felt his glance on her she smiled up at him, the dancing flames of the fire reflected in her eyes. She was wishing that she hadn't let him tune into her earlier melancholy. The occasion may have belonged to Montrose and Tabitha, but these were special moments for the two of them as well. They were together and in the joy of it she didn't want either the past or the future to intrude.

Tabitha was dressed in a wedding gown similar to those Anna had seen in the magazine that time and Montrose was in a black jacket with a cut-away front, white embroidered shirt, a bright neckerchief, and tight black trousers to finish the ensemble.

As the bridal couple made their vows in front of them all and Marco watched from inside the caravan, there was silence from the onlookers as they each said just a few simple words, declaring their love and promising to be faithful.

Once it was over the men blew their noses, the women wiped their eyes and the musicians struck up from behind as the festivities began. A roasted pig had been lifted off the spit and large platters of fried potatoes and vegetables stuffed with meat and herbs were passed round as the pork was carved by two of the men.

When Anna and Glenn went to congratulate the newlyweds, Tabitha smiled shyly and Montrose thanked them for the gift and said to Glenn, 'Thank you also for taking care of my father.'

He smiled. 'I was only doing my job.'

Anna and Glenn had enjoyed the food and drank the wine and now they were dancing a lively jig around the fire with other energetic members of the wedding guests. The frosty night on the edge of the warm circle that encompassed them was forgotten, Everything was centred on the fire and the music and as Glenn held her close while they danced he knew that he could never contemplate a life without her.

But he was aware that she wasn't prepared to take up where they'd left off when he'd first gone to Africa. She had been the one to end their relationship on that ghastly day when he'd come to find out why she hadn't kept to her promise to join him, and now that he'd come to Willowmere for one last time and seen what her life was like it seemed obvious that it was the children that had kept her there.

She'd told him at the time about the accident where she'd been injured and James's wife had been killed, but she had seemed to have made a full recovery and he'd taken it all at face value. Maybe he shouldn't have, but Anna's determination to end their relationship had been unmistakable and he'd left with the future a bleak and empty place.

'Hey!' she said laughingly, bringing him back to earth. 'What are you thinking about? You've gone all serious.'

'Sorry,' he said. Quickening his step he smiled down at her and whirled her round and round in the firelight until she was breathless. When the music stopped he said softly, 'Are you happy, Anna, *really* happy in the life you lead?'

'Yes. Most of the time,' she said slowly, resisting the

desire to tell him that happiness came in different shapes and depths, and if he was asking if she ever reached the heights of it the answer was no, not for a long time anyway.

They were coming round with the food again and their glasses were being refilled, and to her relief the moment of questioning passed.

The wedding celebrations were still in full swing when they left at just before midnight, and would go on for a few days until someone called a halt. At that point Tabitha's womenfolk would unbraid her hair before her new husband took her to live with his parents in their caravan, and her mother-in-law would cover her head with the scarf that she must now always wear in public.

'That was fantastic,' Glenn said as they strolled home beneath the same winter moon that had been reflected in the lake on the night that he'd found her there in solitary contemplation.

'Mmm, it was,' she murmured dreamily. 'The gypsies have some lovely customs, don't they?'

'Such as this,' he said laughingly as he took her in his arms and danced her along the main street of the village, past the fairy-lights in the windows of the cottages, past the giant Christmas tree in the square where the surgery was, and up the path of the place she called home.

As they faced each other breathlessly at her door Anna wanted to stay in his arms for ever, with every-thing open and truthful between them. But it was still there, the fear that he would want to marry her out of concern rather than desire if she ever told him what had happened to her.

Sensing that she was retreating behind the wariness that never seemed to go away, he kissed her just once with a tenderness and passion that made her bones melt and then, releasing her, said, 'Love and marriage are so simple for the people we've just been with. I wish it was that easy for you and I.' And she thought he had no idea how near the truth he was.

Taking the door key out of her hand, he unlocked the door of the annexe and as she stepped inside he said, 'Thanks for a wonderful experience.' And went striding off to where Bracken House stood in the darkness of the midnight hour.

As she bolted the door behind him Anna thought that Glenn had made no attempt to follow her into the place where they could have been alone and private, but perhaps it was just as well. When he'd danced her home the night had been charged with romance and desire and it would have been so easy to forget everything but their need of each other.

Releasing the clasp of the bright shawl she'd worn, she draped it over the back of a chair and went into the kitchen to make a hot drink, and when she looked out of the window he was standing motionless beneath the streetlamp as if reluctant to go into his temporary ac-commodation. When she looked again he'd gone and, taking the drink with her, she went slowly up to bed.

Clare Halliday's results from her blood tests were back on Monday morning and Anna thought if Georgina's expression was anything to go by as she studied them there was distress ahead for the owner of the art gallery. As if to give substance to the premonition, Georgina asked one of the receptionists to ring Clare and ask her to come in as soon as possible.

The two nurses exchanged glances and when they were alone Beth said, 'Whatever it is that's wrong, Clare can do without it at this moment in time. Her mother is very demanding and difficult to deal with. If she has a serious health problem, I don't know how she'll cope.'

They were getting ready for the antenatal clinic at the time and Clare's problems were shelved for a while as the young mothers and a radiant Maggie Timmins came to be checked over by Georgina and helped by the nurses with any worries they might have.

When Anna told the poultry farmer's wife that her blood pressure was up, she groaned in dismay and asked, 'So what do I have to do to bring it down?'

'Rest, rest and more rest,' she told her firmly.

'All right,' she agreed, 'but it won't be easy. There is always so much to do on the farm.'

'Yes, I know,' Anna said, 'but you'll just have to ignore it. If your blood pressure goes any higher, we might have to admit you to hospital for complete bed rest until the birth. Hypertension later in the pregnancy is one of the causes of pre-eclampsia, which can be life-threatening.'

'But I'm only four months,' she protested.

'Yes, I know, but we still can't ignore high blood pressure, even at this stage. You don't want anything to happen to your baby, do you?'

'Heaven forbid!' she exclaimed. 'Josh is thrilled at the thought of having a baby brother or sister, and Bryan is falling over himself to make a nursery out of the smallest bedroom.'

'So feet up,' Anna told her. 'We are going to make sure they aren't disappointed.'

As the last of the mothers-to-be was leaving, Glenn was coming back from his home visits and he waved as he went into his room. They'd met briefly first thing during the breakfast rush but neither had referred to Saturday's events.

Anna because every time she thought about how he'd danced her through the village and his farewell kiss she went weak at the knees, and he had the sort of look about him that said that had been Saturday and today was another day.

She wasn't to know that he too hadn't stopped thinking about the wedding and afterwards.

When she'd gone in at breakfast-time to get the children ready for school he'd been in the shower and she'd asked James if Glenn had mentioned the wedding. 'Only briefly,' he'd said, 'but I took it that it had been quite something. We've been discussing the practice mostly over the weekend and Glenn has been telling me about his time abroad. He mentioned that you were just as keen as he was at the time. I do wish I'd known. You should have told me.'

'It didn't matter,' she'd said flatly. 'I was needed here, in case you've forgotten.'

He'd smiled apologetically. 'Of course I haven't forgotten. Having you here saved my sanity, but you deserve to fulfill your dreams just as much as anyone else. If you just said the word, maybe it would be your own wedding you'd be going to, and people in need of medical aid around the world would welcome the two of you with open arms.'

She'd been uptight then. 'There is a certain matter of a major operation I had to have at that time, which is one of the reasons why I can't do that. And what about the children?' As he'd stared at her in dismay because he'd upset her, she'd asked, 'Is their dinner money ready?' Then, regretting her momentary annoyance, she went on, 'I'm sorry, James. It must be the Monday morning blues that are getting to me.'

'I'm sorry too,' he'd said mildly, 'but all I want is that you should be happy, and how do you know that Glenn won't be able to cope with you being unable to give him children?'

She'd sighed. 'You have your answer to that in the way he is with yours. Can you imagine what he would be like with children of his own?'

And now as she and Beth cleared away after the clinic and Clare came hurrying through the main doors with her face a white mask of anxiety, the memory of what James had said was still there in her mind.

It wasn't until the children came out of school that reason asserted itself. Their faces lit up as they always did when they saw her waiting. Life was good, life was normal, she told herself as she hugged them to her and, as sometimes happened, she had a sense of Julie's presence nearby, gentle and reassuring.

She wished they could have a chat, she thought sombrely, so that she could tell the sister-in-law that she'd loved so much how her heartstrings were being pulled in so many ways.

# CHAPTER EIGHT

WHEN Anna and the children arrived at Bracken House, Clare was leaving the surgery after her consultation with Georgina, and with head bowed and shoulders drooping she was the picture of dejection.

She looked up as the children's chatter drifted across and managed a smile as the three of them approached.

'So how did it go, Clare?' Anna asked in low-voiced concern.

'Dr Adams is arranging for me to see an oncologist,' she said in flat tones. 'There are indications that I might have ovarian cancer. I hope they don't keep me waiting too long before I get a diagnosis.'

'Oh, dear, that *is* upsetting news!' Anna commiserated. 'But try to think positive until they have something definite to tell you, and if it is what they think it might be, cancer treatments are improving by the minute. What are you going to tell your mother?'

'Nothing, I think, until I know for sure. I brought Mum to live with me so that I could look after her. A lot of use I'm going to be if I have to have surgery and chemotherapy.'

'Clare, you have friends here who will want to be

there for you, me for one, so take comfort from that, and as Christmas is so near, try to put every other thought from your mind but the pleasant ones. You have the best voice of all of us when we go carol singing, we can't manage without you.'

The off-the-cuff therapy seemed to be working as Clare's expression brightened at the compliment. 'I won't let you down,' she promised, 'and, please, don't mention my problem to anyone, will you?'

'No, of course not,' she assured her, and as they each went their separate ways she thought that ill health and sadness didn't disappear just because it was Christmas.

That was the downbeat part of the day. When Anna answered the doorbell shortly after they'd eaten their evening meal, she was delighted to see Beth's daughter, Jess, standing in the porch, smiling at her.

Jess had a carrier bag with her and whispered, 'Presents for Polly and Jolly. Where shall I put them?'

Anna opened the door of a nearby cupboard and said, 'In there. They'll be here in a moment if they've heard your voice.'

The children were thrilled to see Jess again, and while she played patiently with them she brought Anna and James up to date with what was going on in her life.

'I'm still looking for a job,' she told them, 'and have had a few offers, but none of them are local and I don't want to move away, so I'm leaving it until after Christmas now, which means if you need a sitter I'll be available.'

'What about next week when the children have finished school for the Christmas holiday?' James suggested. 'It would allow Anna to be at the surgery instead of having to take time off, and would help your finances, Jess.'

'Yes!' she said immediately. 'That would be great. I could cover the week after Christmas too if you want, and then I really will have to get organised on the job scene.'

While Jess was upstairs with the children James said, 'I hope you didn't mind me snapping Jess up for the next two weeks and bringing you into the surgery. It seemed a shame not to take advantage of her being free.'

'No, of course I don't mind,' she told him. 'It will be some extra practice for Jess before she starts work. And like you said it means some extra money for her over the holiday.'

He nodded. 'When she finds herself a job, some children somewhere will be very fortunate.'

As the night of the Mistletoe Ball drew near, Anna thought it was turning out to be a strange week full of highs and lows. Clare's worrying condition and Glenn's restrained manner every time they met at the surgery or during the breakfast rush were amongst the lows, while Jess's appearance came top of the highs.

When she was about to collect the children on Friday afternoon he said, as if it had been the main topic of conversation between them during the week, 'What time shall I call for you tomorrow?'

Feigning puzzlement she asked, 'Why, are we going somewhere?'

There was a glint in the dark blue gaze looking into hers that told her he'd got the message, and unperturbed he said, 'Surely you haven't forgotten. You are going to the ball, Cinderella.'

'Oh, *that*. You got the tickets then?'

'I would have said if I hadn't,' he informed her dryly. 'So what time shall I call for you?'

The low-key approach wasn't working, he thought. It was something he'd decided on after the gypsy wedding in the hope that a lack of response on his part might bring what was in Anna's mind out into the open. The wedding had been the sort of occasion that dreams were made of, but there was still that same caution in her manner whenever they got close, and he wished he could get to the bottom of it.

The more he saw of it the more he felt that James and the children weren't the cause of it. Maybe it was just him who didn't fit into her permanent scheme of things. That he was all right to have around but that she hadn't changed her mind about what she'd said to him when she'd told him it was over.

But it was agony being aloof and it certainly wasn't bringing Anna flying into his arms. He'd probably blown it and she'd decided not to go. So where did they go from this point?

But she was saying, 'Eight o'clock, if that's all right with you.'

'Fine,' he said with assumed easiness. 'I'm looking forward to giving the dress suit an airing,' and went back to his patients.

It being Christmas and the last day of term, the children came out of school holding Christmas cards that they'd made for James and herself and clutching the presents they'd been given by Santa, the elderly school caretaker who had dressed for the occasion. Suddenly the realisation of how near it was hit her.

All the things that she loved about this time of year in Willowmere were about to happen. The ball tomorrow night was the first and there was no way she wanted to put the blight on that for the two of them because of her confused feelings about Glenn.

James had the chance to go with them now that Jess was available and she wished he would. His social life was almost non-existent. She suggested it when he came in at the end of the day but he said, 'No. I haven't got a partner, for one thing. I had some offers but didn't take them up. All I want is for you to enjoy yourself with Glenn.'

There was a dress in the wardrobe that she hadn't yet worn with a cream strapless bodice and a full black skirt with cream flounces around the hemline. She'd been saving it for something special and couldn't think of a more fitting occasion than the Mistletoe Ball.

It would be another time when she was pretending that all was right between them and she knew it couldn't go on. That sooner or later Glenn would want to know where they were heading, but not tonight, she prayed. Please, not tonight.

When Glenn came for her he was carrying an oblong box and as she stepped back to let him in he said, 'I took the liberty of bringing you a corsage. I didn't know what you'd be wearing so thought that cream roses would be the safest thing. Now I see that it was an inspired guess.'

As she opened the box and looked down at the flowers inside, the uncertainties of the last few days disappeared, and when she raised her head and met his glance she was happy to see that his coolness of the past week had gone.

'The dress is stunning,' he said. 'Is it new?'

'I've had it a while but never worn it,' she told him. 'I've been waiting for the right moment. And by the way, the suit looks all right.'

He looked more than 'all right', she thought. There would be a few heads turning when they presented themselves at the ball, and they would be aimed in his direction rather than hers.

When she lifted the corsage out of the box he said, 'Shall I fasten it on for you? I've got some large pins.' When she nodded, overcome by the unexpectedness of the moment, he pointed out, 'We do have a problem, though. There are no straps or shoulder pieces to fasten it to. Shall I fix it horizontally across the top of the bodice?'

'Yes, whatever you think best,' she agreed, as if she was incapable of fixing it herself, and as he did as he'd suggested, she tried to ignore his touch against the top of her breasts as he pinned it from the inside.

'Sorry about that,' he said, as if her awareness of his hands against her body had been noted. 'Another time I would need to check out the dress before I order the flowers.'

*Would there be another time?* she wondered as he took the stole that matched the dress from her, draped it around her shoulders, then swivelled her round to face him. As their eyes met, his guard was down. She saw what she wanted to see there.

But as if on cue the doorbell rang once more and this time it was James and the children come to wish them a nice time at the ball, and when they'd gone so had the moment that they'd broken into.

As soon as they stepped out of the door Anna and Glenn could hear the music coming from the marquee on the school playing fields, and as they walked the short distance along with others going in the same direction, she was smiling at the thought of how different the music would be the following night when the band struck up with the age-old carols that people loved so much.

Glenn had seen the smile and asked, 'What's amusing you?' He'd placed her hand in the crook of his arm in case it was icy underfoot, and as he looked down at her he was wondering just how long he could keep up the pretence of being content to be on the edge of her life when he ached for her so much.

'I was thinking that tonight the music is going to be for ballroom and modern dancing,' she explained. 'In sharp contrast tomorrow night, we'll have the brass band playing carols.'

'I am really looking forward to that,' he declared. 'If I hadn't lost my trumpet, I'd be asking if I could join them.'

'Yes, it's a shame,' she said. She'd been late-night shopping on her own the other night and had bought a trumpet that was as near to the one he'd lost as she could get, and once that had been done had asked Jack from the post office, who was in charge of the band, if Glenn might join in the practice they would be having in the afternoon before the carol singing.

'Aye!' he'd said. 'We're short on trumpets since the Belshaw brothers retired to the seaside.'

'I've bought him one as a gift,' she'd told him. 'It's going to be a surprise. His original instrument was lost while he was abroad.'

'Eh, up!' he'd exclaimed. 'That's some present. How did you know what to get?'

She'd laughed. 'We were a threesome once—Glenn, me and his trumpet.'

'Ah, I see,' he'd said meaningfully, and she'd become serious.

'Don't read anything into it, Jack. We're just friends from way back.'

'That's a pity. The wife thinks he's a big improvement on the male talent in the village and says if she was twenty years younger…'

'Although he's enchanted with Willowmere, Glenn is drawn to working abroad. He may not be with us long.' She'd said it lightly, yet the mere thought of him disappearing out of her life again was unbearable.

If the accident hadn't happened, Julie would have been there for her children and she, Anna, would have been able to give Glenn the family that he longed for. She would have joined him in Africa as arranged and they would have been married by now, maybe already with children of their own.

Why was nothing ever simple? she'd wondered as she'd gone home to gift-wrap the shining instrument.

This time as they danced it was a more sedate exercise than the jigs around the fire at the gypsy wedding, and as the evening progressed, with friends and acquaintances all around them, Glenn thought that, apart from her feeling of responsibility towards the children, there was this closely bound community that Anna would never want to leave to work in a foreign country. He didn't set such store on himself as to imagine she would give all this up for *him*.

He knew that eyes were on them, that people must be wondering what was going on between Anna and the new doctor, and if they should ask, the answer was not a lot.

Georgina was there with a blond guy that she seemed to be on good terms with. Beth and her husband had just swayed past, doing a tango, and Bill Bradshaw, the farmer who'd sold Anna the tree and had since been to consult him about a prostate problem, was there with his wife. And everywhere amongst the festive gathering was mistletoe, the kissing bough.

Lots of folk were laughingly taking advantage of the opportunity to exchange Christmas kisses beneath the smooth green leaves with their clusters of white berries, and to his surprise Anna reached up and kissed him fleetingly when they passed beneath them while dancing.

'What have I done to deserve that?' he asked in a low voice.

'It was just to say merry Christmas,' she said lightly.

And he thought wryly, *In other words, don't get any wrong ideas*.

He didn't dance her through the village as they returned home this time. They moved sedately amongst the homeward-bound throng and when they reached her door she said, 'Would you like to come inside for a moment?'

'Why would you want me to do that?' he asked.

'You'll understand when you do.' Taking his hand, she pulled him into the lighted hallway and through into the sitting room, where he stood observing her questioningly.

'I have something for you,' she said. 'If you'll excuse me for a second, I'll go and get it.'

'Er, yes,' he replied, taken aback. 'Though I can't think what it could be.'

She was smiling. 'That is how I want you to feel. Close your eyes and don't open them until I say so.'

He heard her leave the room and seconds later she was back and telling him, 'You can open them now.' As he did so she thrust a bulky package into his hands and said, 'Happy Christmas, Glenn.'

'Thank you, Anna,' he said slowly, 'but why so soon?'

'Open it and you'll find out why.'

When he saw the trumpet shining brassily up at him in its case he was dumbstruck and for a few seconds there was silence until, finding his voice, he said huskily, 'You bought this for *me*, and gave it to me now so that I can play tomorrow if they'll have me.'

'They'll have you all right,' she assured him. 'Once they hear you play, the band with think that Christmas has come early for them as well.'

He was stroking the shining metal with loving fingers. 'This is the nicest, kindest thing anyone has ever done for me, Anna, and I assure you that wherever I am, *this* will never get lost because *you* gave it to me.'

'So you really aren't intending to stay?' she asked, tears pricking as the moment lost its magic.

He bent and kissed her brow. 'Whatever happens I

want us to have this Christmas together, and when, or I should say *if* you hear me play with the band tomorrow, I will be playing for you alone.'

He called late on Sunday afternoon and said triumphantly, 'I've just been to the band practice and will be playing with them tonight. They've accepted me on a temporary basis after I explained that I wasn't sure how long I was going to be around. Great stuff, eh, Anna?'

'Yes, if it makes you happy,' she told him, touched by his enthusiasm but with a heavy heart. 'Are you going to the candlelit service first?'

'Yes, of course. What about you and the family?'

'We'll be there. The children are going to stay up late for once, but James will bring them home after the service. It will be a few years before they're old enough to go carol singing.'

He turned away. She was referring to the future, a future that wouldn't include him, and he couldn't face the role of onlooker for the rest of his life.

When he'd found Anna still living in Willowmere and leading a very different kind of life to his, he'd thought he would be able to wait until she turned to him even if it took for ever. But it wasn't turning out as easy as that and he'd decided that he was going to live for the moment and if that and the trumpet were all he had to take with him when he left, it would have to be enough.

The old stone church was packed for the special service that always filled its pews and as the five of them sat together, waiting for it to start, Anna thought that everyone she loved was there beside her.

There was James, patient and loving, next to Pollyanna, who was wide-eyed and excited to see the crib in front of the altar and the many candles flickering. Beside her was Jolyon, trying to keep awake, and on Anna's other side was the man who had come back into her life and given it meaning. Glenn, strong, caring, needing her, wanting her, yet she couldn't say the words in her heart.

'There's Jess waving to us,' Polly said, bringing Anna's thoughts back to the moment, and as they waved back she saw Clare and her mother seated nearby.

When she smiled across, her mother nodded graciously and Anna wondered how she would cope if her daughter's fears were realised. But tonight was about happier things than that, and as Clare's voice rang out amongst the carol singers later in the evening, maybe she would be able to forget everything but the pleasure of singing.

As the service progressed, Anna turned to look at the man by her side and there was such warmth in the glance meeting hers that she felt like weeping for all the time they'd lost.

'What?' he asked in a low voice when he saw that her eyes were moist.

'Nothing,' she whispered back. 'I was just thinking about us, that's all.'

'And it makes you cry? That is the last thing I would want.'

'Maybe,' she parried, 'but we don't always get what we want, do we?'

James had taken the children home, the hot mince pies and coffee at the vicarage had been enjoyed, and now

Glenn had gone to join the band assembling outside in readiness for the march around the village to play for those who hadn't been able to get to the service.

The carol singers were carrying lanterns to light up the hymn sheets they were holding and as a waning moon shone down onto the brass of the instruments and cast shadows along the way, the spirit of Christmas was all around them.

Every time they stopped outside a house Anna's glance was on Glenn, with the trumpet to his lips, and she smiled. At least she'd done one thing to bring him joy.

As the words and music sounded out on the frosty night air she knew that the only thing she would ever want to leave this enchanted place for would be to fulfill her dream of going to help the less fortunate people of the world with Glenn by her side, but that was not on her agenda, it couldn't be, though it might be on his.

They'd been asked to sing at one of the farms and had been plied with mulled wine and hotpot, and Glenn's continuing introduction to country life had once again had him amazed. 'I can't believe how hospitable the people in Willowmere are,' he said as they walked home after the singing was over.

'You should see the show of strength when one of us has sickness or sorrow to contend with, or is lonely or hurt,' she told him. 'As soon as the news gets around, everyone rallies, anxious to do all they can to make life more bearable. So you see what you'll be missing if you don't stay,' she said lightly.

'I know what I'll be missing,' he told her, 'and it won't just be the community spirit that I see everywhere I go. But let's not get onto a taboo subject.

Tonight has been another fantastic occasion. Everything about it has been great, and I owe it all to you, Anna. Not only that, I've played the trumpet again for the first time in ages, and you were there to hear me play. What more could I ask?'

They were home. Any moment Glenn was going to leave her again and she didn't want him to, but he surprised her by saying, 'How about inviting me in for a hot toddy or something similarly warming?' As she stepped back to let him in he said, 'The frost tonight is intense. Do you think the lake will freeze over this winter?'

'It might. I've skated on it a few times and it's exhilarating, but one has to watch out for a sudden thaw, it can be dangerous then.'

'I wouldn't mind having a go if it does freeze,' he said.

'James has some spare skates you could borrow.'

'I'll bear that in mind.'

They were chatting easily enough, Anna thought, in these intimate moments together as they sipped the warming liquid and she said, 'You know the band won't let you go now that they've heard you play. It was like old times, watching and listening to you.'

He was smiling. 'I don't know how you put up with me in those days.'

'Rubbish! It was great,' she told him, and didn't confess that ever since she'd sent him away, she'd wanted to weep buckets every time she heard a trumpet played. *Until today, that was.*

Glenn was getting to his feet and the magical night was about to end. Anna knew she had only to say the word and he would stay. They would make love and it would like it used to be, passionate and tender, but it would be giving him hope where there wasn't any, and she couldn't do that to him.

When she arrived at the surgery on Monday morning, he observed her questioningly. 'Who have you left the children with?' he asked.

'Jess,' she told him. 'James asked her if she would mind them for this week and next so that I could be here, and she was keen to do so.' She was taking in the scene before her. 'What's happening here? I see that we have a very full waiting room.'

'Georgina has booked a couple of days off to do some Christmas shopping, so that is slowing things down, plus coughs and colds seem to be the order of the day, which makes your presence most welcome.'

It was welcome any time, he was thinking, but even more so today. He'd resigned himself to not seeing much of Anna in these last few days before Christmas and here she was, already calling in her first patient from outside the nurses' room, and he returned to his own duties with a smile on his face.

When he went outside to start his home visits the sky was grey, clouds were lower over the peaks and the cold was intense. He'd strolled down to the lake first thing before presenting himself at the surgery and had seen that there was still some slight movement of the water, but if the cold increased there was a chance that it would freeze over.

On a bleak winter morning Willow Lake had not been at its best and one of the council workmen that he'd found festooning the trees around it with fairy-lights had said, 'It'll look better tonight, when these are switched on.'

No doubt it would, he'd thought, and the memory of the night he'd found Anna there had surfaced. They'd had the place to themselves, but for what good it had done it may as well have been crowded.

As he'd passed the gypsy site on his way to the lake he'd seen that Montrose and his people were still there, and even though it had been early, a couple of the men had been outside the caravans, chopping up fallen tree trunks for the fire. They'd waved and he'd waved back, and wondered how Tabitha was coping with her new status.

The memory of the wedding would stay with him for ever—the food, the music, dancing in the light from the fire with Anna in his arms happy and relaxed. Would he be able to stay calm and controlled all over Christmas when every time he was near her the longing to have her permanently in his life took him by the throat?

As he drove up the road to the moors to visit the elderly mother of one of the sheep farmers, his thoughts were still sombre. He was here, in the place where he could see Anna, touch her, work with her and socialize with her, yet he was no nearer to knowing what went on in her mind. One moment she was how he wanted her to be—happy in his company, loving and thought-ful as when she'd bought him the trumpet—and the next withdrawn into some private place of her own that he wasn't allowed to enter.

If he had any sense he would pack his bags and go as speedily as he had come. The opposition he faced was not so much lack of interest on Anna's part, or someone of his own sex that she preferred to him. It might be easier to accept if it was.

It was what had happened in the past that had driven them apart. He'd been waiting impatiently for her to join him in Africa and had been faced with silence, no communication of any kind, and he'd come to find out why.

That had been when he'd discovered that James's wife had been killed and Anna injured in a car crash with the twin babies in the car who miraculously had been unhurt.

She had looked dreadful, but before he'd been able to express his concern about her wellbeing and the tragedy that had befallen her brother, she'd been sending him on his way, telling him bluntly that their romance was over because her future responsibilities were going to be with James and his family, and even when he'd said that he would come back and they could live nearby, she had still been adamant that it was over.

# CHAPTER NINE

WHILE Glenn was thinking sombre thoughts James was having a pleasant surprise. An old friend had returned unexpectedly to the village after six years' absence and had called in at the surgery to see him.

Helen Martin had been his parents' housekeeper for many years before she'd gone to live in Canada to be near her daughter, and now it seemed that she was back and living in a new apartment block recently erected on the outskirts of the village.

'I was so sorry to learn that you've lost both your parents,' she said when he showed her into his consulting room, '*and* your lovely wife, James. I only moved in yesterday but I was soon brought up to date with what has been going on in my absence. You have twin children, I believe, and Anna lives with you.'

He smiled wryly. 'You've been informed correctly, Helen. Anna put her own affairs to one side to help me look after my children when Julie died. She's been living next door to us ever since and, believe me, there have been times when the two of us would have been over the moon to have you back at Bracken House. Are you home for good?'

The robust middle-aged woman seated opposite nodded her head. 'Yes. I was homesick and my daughter and her brood didn't need me any more, so here I am, turning up like a bad penny, and I don't mind telling you it's great to be back.'

'It's great to *have* you back,' he assured her, and asked, 'Am I to take it that this is just a social call? You haven't got any health problems?'

'No. I'm fine, you'll be relieved to know. I just called in to renew our acquaintance.'

'You must have a word with Anna while you're here,' he told her. 'She'll be delighted to see you.'

Anna was. 'Helen!' she cried, flinging her arms around the housekeeper. 'I don't believe it! Please, tell me that you've come back.'

'I have,' she was told. 'I'm here to stay. I was homesick for Willowmere, Anna. So here I am.'

'You have no idea how many times I've wished you were here,' Anna told her. 'So much has happened since you left.'

'And what about *your* life?' Helen asked sympathetically. 'No husband or fiancé around?'

Anna shook her head and the smooth red-gold of her hair moved gently with the motion. 'No. I help to look after the children and am a part-time nurse at the surgery, which doesn't leave much time for anything else.'

'I can believe that,' the unexpected visitor said. 'Who is minding the children today?'

'A young friend of ours, Jess.'

'I'd love to see them. Is it all right if I pop round some time?'

'Of course it is. Are you retired now?'

'I'm supposed to be, but I have too much energy to be lazing around. I shall look for something in the village, I think, when I've settled in.'

James came to seek her out when Helen had gone and said, 'What about that, Helen turning up unexpectedly? Wasn't it great to see her and to know she's back where she belongs? Mum and Dad thought the world of her, didn't they?'

'Yes, they did, and so did we,' she said fondly. 'I'll never forget her amazing cooking either.'

'What does she intend doing with herself now she's back? Did she say?'

'She's going to look for something in the village once she's settled in.'

'Really?' he commented, and went back to his own domain in a thoughtful mood.

Anna left the surgery at five o'clock to relieve Jess and to prepare their evening meal, leaving Glenn and James still occupied with the last patients of the day who had come on late appointments after work. When she put her key in the lock of Bracken House, she had the strangest feeling.

It was as if she'd moved on a step by trusting someone else to look after Pollyanna and Jolyon for so many hours. As if the loving bond that bound her to them had become less tight, yet without any loss to them.

When she opened the door the three of them were in the hall, waiting to greet her, and the children's expressions told her that all was well. 'How has it gone?' she asked Jess. 'Any problems?'

She was smiling. 'No, Anna. We've had a great time,

haven't we, children?' she asked them, and they both nodded enthusiastically.

'We went to the park this morning, had a little rest after lunch and then played games,' she said. Bending to kiss their cheeks, she reminded them that she would be with them again the next day.

Jess waved to them from the gate and as they all waved back Anna saw Glenn coming up the path, and the first thing he said when he came in was to ask how the childminding had gone.

'Fine,' she told him, aware that they hadn't seen much of each other during the day. It had been so busy, and he'd been out longer than usual on a full list of house calls. As he stood beside her she saw that he had a sort of closed-up, defeated look about him that made her reach out to take his hand.

'Don't!' he said abruptly, and as her arm fell away he turned and went up to his room without further comment.

'I've just seen Police Constable Jarvis,' James said when he got home a few minutes later. 'He says that the lake is frozen solid and some youngsters were already on their way there with their skates as he came through the village. So he's going to need eyes in the back of his head while it's in that state. He's been in touch with the council and they're going to transfer one of the park wardens there in the morning to patrol the lake in case of any accidents and to put up danger notices so that anyone skating there will take care.'

'Is he sure that it's safe now?' she asked absently, still smarting from Glenn's unexpected rejection.

'Yes. He's tried it himself and it's solid, but a frozen surface can change from one second to the next and just a short time in freezing cold water can be fatal. If you want to enjoy one of your favourite pastimes, I suggest you go tonight.'

'What, in the dark?'

'No. Glenn reckons that he was there this morning and the council workers were putting coloured lights on the trees around the lake so I can see half the village being there.'

'Can he borrow your spare skates?' she asked. 'He's keen to try it out.'

'Tell him, yes, my pleasure.'

When the children were asleep and James was doing some odd jobs around the house, Anna went next door to change into trousers, a warm jacket, woolly hat and scarf, and with a pair of skates dangling from her hand she came back to find Glenn.

'The lake is frozen over,' she announced when she found him alone in the sitting room while James was getting the children ready for bed. 'Are you still in a bad mood, or do we go skating?'

'I am not in a bad mood,' he replied, 'and, yes, we go skating, if James will lend me his skates.'

'He will.'

'Then you'd better take a seat while I find some suitable clothes,' he said, and thought he didn't deserve this after being so abrupt earlier.

'I'm sorry I snapped at you,' he told her when he appeared dressed in a similar manner to herself. 'You didn't deserve it.'

'Don't fret about it,' she said. 'I was worried about you, though I didn't mean to fuss. Shall we forget it?'

He was smiling now. 'Yes, please.'

James's prediction was correct. There were lots of villagers on the ice in the winter paradise that the council had created and as they joined them, holding hands, all their uncertainties disappeared in the exhilaration of gliding along together.

It was almost midnight when they left and there were still some people there, but tomorrow was another working day for them and hopefully the ice would still be there the following evening.

'How long since the lake last froze over?' Glenn asked as they walked home.

'A few years, maybe eight or nine,' she told him. 'It was when I came home from university one Christmas and found it the centre of attraction for everyone.'

'Tonight will be another happy memory to go on my list,' he said as the house and surgery came into view.

Now it was her turn to be touchy. 'Every time you say something nice, there is a hidden reminder in it that you are not going to be here long,' she said stiffly. 'Do you get a kick out of torturing me? The situation I'm in is something I didn't ask for, but was dealing with contentedly enough until you came back into my life, and now I'm being pulled all ways. You make me feel as if I'm being deliberately difficult all the time. How would *you* feel if we were married and I died and left you with two newborn babies to bring up? Wouldn't you be glad of the help of your sister if you had one?'

She wasn't being truthful. James and the children

would cope without her if they had to. The real reason was locked away in her heart and there it had to stay.

'Shush!' he commanded, turning to face her. 'Do you think I don't understand what it's like for you, Anna? But if I go back to where I've come from, it will be because I'll know once and for all that it really is over between us as far as you're concerned.'

There were tears on her lashes and he wiped them away gently with the ends of her scarf. 'Three more days and it will be Christmas Eve and if I promise not to mention leaving again, will you promise not to shed any more tears?'

'Yes,' she said with a watery smile. 'I promise.'

'Come on, then, I'll race you to the front gate. If I remember rightly, you used to be quite a sprinter.'

They arrived together laughing and breathless, but as they separated it was there again, the sadness and the longing. When she was almost at her front door Glenn called her name across the surgery forecourt and she stopped. He was by her side in seconds and as she observed him questioningly he took her face between his two hands and kissed her gently on the mouth. When he released her he said softly, 'Thanks for worrying about me earlier. I can't remember when last anyone did that.' And before she'd got over her surprise he'd gone.

The skating on the lake continued the next day under the watchful eyes of the park warden and in the evening, after they'd finished their meal, James suggested, 'Why don't you and Glenn take the children to watch the skating, Anna? I'll tidy up here.'

'No,' she said, 'you take them with Glenn, James.

You haven't seen the lake lit up. It's like fairyland. *I'll* do the clearing away.' But he was insistent that it was she and Glenn who took them, and she had a feeling that he wanted her out of the way, though he'd said he might join them later.

'I'm sure Glenn would rather be with you than me,' he commented. 'It's clear to see how he feels about you, but are you in love with him, Anna? He told me today that you bought him a trumpet for Christmas and he was over the moon when he told me. I don't mean to inter-fere, but a relationship that is one-sided is going no-where.'

'Yes, I bought him a trumpet,' she said evenly. 'And, yes, I do love him. I know that now. I've always loved him, I always will, but if there is one thing that Glenn wants out of life it is a family, children of his own. He had a haphazard sort of upbringing and until he came to Willowmere and came to live here he had no experi-ence of family life, which makes him even more keen to create one of his own. But, as we both know, I can't give him the children that he wants so badly and there is no way I want to put him in a position where he has to choose between me and them.' As she finally spoke her true feelings out loud, Anna realised just how much she really did love Glenn. And just how futile that love was.

James did see. Saw only too clearly that he could at least put Anna's mind at rest regarding his affairs, and while she and Glenn were at the lake with the children he was going to take the first step towards that end by visiting a newly erected apartment on the outskirts of Willowmere.

That would his first move. The second would be to

call at a converted barn just five minutes' walk away. In both instances he would be hoping that the plans that he'd been turning over in his mind during recent days might take shape.

Glenn came downstairs a little later and asked, 'Are we going to the lake again, Anna?'

Yes,' she told him. 'James wants us to take the children to see the skating.'

'Great! They'll like that,' he exclaimed, and within minutes the four of them were on their way to Willow Lake. When they got there Anna saw Clare and thought that the other woman was doing what she'd advised— to hold her worries at bay, keeping herself occupied. Clare had led the carol singers on Sunday night, as promised, and now was enjoying local winter sports. Perhaps some time over Christmas they could get together for a coffee or a glass of wine.

'You'll have to give the children skating lessons before the next time the lake freezes over, Anna. Kids of their age will soon pick it up,' Glenn said as they stood at the edge of the ice.

And she thought that it was there again, the 'I won't be around' message in what he'd just said.

She was holding tightly to the twins' hands and said with assumed nonchalance, 'Polly, the impetuous, is champing at the bit already, but Jolly is weighing up the ice with his usual caution. If I thought it would last, I would persuade James to get them kitted out with skates now, but the weather forecast indicates that temperatures could rise in the next few days.'

She was looking around her. 'I see that the notices

are up advising caution with regard to thin ice. Where's the park warden who is keeping an eye on things?'

'I've just heard someone say that he's been called to an incident on the river a couple of miles away so that is the last we'll see of him today. He would have been due to finish when the emergency arose, so I'm going to stay until everyone has gone. I had some experience of water rescue while I was abroad and have a grasp of the basics, but there is no sign of a thaw as yet.'

She shuddered. 'It's a gruesome thought, someone falling through the ice.'

'Yes. Especially as children and teenagers are the ones who respond to this kind of excitement the most, and the council can't afford to have a park warden on duty twenty-four hours a day.'

James appeared at that moment and she asked, 'Have you brought your skates?'

'Yes,' he said. 'I knew I wouldn't be able to resist it once I saw the ice, but Jolly is rubbing his eyes, bedtime is calling. Maybe another day.'

'There mightn't be another time,' Glenn told him. 'Temperatures are forecast to rise.'

'Stay,' Anna urged. 'Glenn has taken over from the park warden so you can keep him company.' And still holding tightly onto the children's hands, she took the little ones home to bed and spent the rest of the evening wrapping Christmas presents and decorating the house with holly and mistletoe.

When James arrived home much later he looked more relaxed than she'd seen him in a long time and she wondered why. Was it the skating, or being with Glenn, or what?

She wished that the future held the prospects of a less lonely life for him, that somewhere there was another woman who could make him as happy as Julie had, but she knew that he didn't think along those lines. He adored his children, enjoyed the challenge of running the practice with dedicated efficiency, and with her beside him seemed to be content.

She'd made a Christmas cake and the following morning got up early to decorate it. It was an average effort, she decided as she covered it in almond paste and thought wistfully of the time when Helen had been in charge of the kitchen and every meal had been something to look forward to.

But it would have to do, and when she'd been to Bryan Timmins's place to pick up the turkey, two of the major food chores of the season would have been accomplished. Or at least they would be once she'd *cooked* the bird!

She'd not seen much of Josh since his finger had healed and hoped that while she was at the farm she might get a glimpse of him, though the odds were that she was more likely to find him skating on the lake than hanging about near home.

It had been her intention to collect the turkey during the lunch-hour, but once she'd had her breakfast she decided to go before she put in an appearance at the surgery as it might be too much of a rush, trying to manage a bite and driving to the farm in the short time that would be available. So when Jess arrived to an enthusiastic welcome from the children, she was ready to leave.

* * *

Glenn's resolve when he'd finished *his* breakfast was along different lines. He did what he'd done the previous day when the lake had become a skating rink—went to check the ice. The temperature *was* rising, the forecast hadn't been wrong, and now was the time for vigilance.

It was barely eight o'clock and only just daylight when he got there. The lights were switched off and he was relieved to see there was no one skating as the park warden hadn't yet arrived.

As he walked around the lake the ice on the edges felt firm enough, but he wondered for how long and hoped that when the warden arrived he would warn any early-morning skaters that it could be dangerous.

He could hear a dog barking not far away and as he looked across the lake he saw a man walking a big golden retriever by the water's edge. It was on a lead and as its owner waved in greeting Glenn waved back and renewed his scrutiny of the ice once more.

Suddenly he heard the man bellow, 'Come back, Goldie! You bad dog!' Glenn looked up to see the dog running across the ice, slithering from side to side as it did so. Its owner was running after it, with the lead dangling from his hand, and the thing he had been concerned about happened. The ice gave way with a resounding crack beneath the man's weight and he plunged into the lake's icy depths as the dog bounded onwards to the other side of the lake and safety.

In the first few moments of dismay Glenn was already springing into action. The warden had brought a throwline with him when he'd started his surveillance and kept it under the seating in a nearby bandstand.

He knew how to use it, Glenn thought desperately, but it needed someone at the other end to pull him in once he'd managed to raise the unfortunate dog-walker out of the water enough to fasten the line round him, and there wasn't a soul in sight.

Anna had to pass the lake on her way to the farm but had no intention of stopping as time was of the essence, until she saw Glenn running from the bandstand with unmistakable urgency and pulling a rope of some sort out of a bag as he ran.

As she turned the car off the road and pulled up at the water's edge, she could hear faint cries for help coming from the centre of the lake where the ice had given way. Someone had fallen through the ice and Glenn was not going to stand by and do nothing, but supposing...

Don't think about it, she told herself. Just help him in any way you can.

When Glenn heard the car drive onto the lakeside he sent up a hasty prayer of thanks, but groaned when he saw who it belonged to. Anna was the last person he wanted involved in this. For one thing, would she have the strength to pull two of them to safety with the line? But there was no time for questioning. If the man was in the water too long, he would either drown or die from hypothermia.

'Thank goodness you're here,' he gasped as he un-ravelled the line and thrust the other end of it into her hands, 'I'm going to crawl across the ice to him, wrap the line around him, and then try to get him out onto where it's still unbroken. Do you think you can pull us to safety?'

'Yes!' she croaked, speaking for the first time since she'd walked into a nightmare.

'Once we are on firm ice I'll be able to drag him along, but first I've got to get him out. OK?'

She'd found her voice now, but there was no time to tell him that if he didn't come out of this alive, she would want to die too, so she just nodded.

Unaware of her anguish, Glenn crawled carefully along the ice to where there was now a large gaping hole. The man's cries were getting fainter, which was ominous, but he closed his mind against what it could mean and, easing himself carefully round to the back of him, reached down into the water.

He could hear the ice cracking all around him and knew that at any time he might fall through it into the icy water. His hands were numb with the cold, but he managed to secure the line around the victim and, putting a hand under each of his armpits, shouted, 'Pull! Pull hard!'

When he looked towards the lakeside he went weak with relief. The warden had turned up and taken charge of the other end of the line, and with Anna's help he began to pull them across the unbroken surface of the lake.

Dry land had never felt more welcome beneath his feet as he staggered onto it, but there was no time to dwell on that or the fact that Anna's face was white with fear. The man he'd brought out of the water needed help and fast.

As far as he could judge his head hadn't been submerged at all which was a miracle. He'd clung on to the edge of the ice and managed to remain upright, but now he was lying motionless, eyes closed, blue with cold, and in spite of the seriousness of his condition would have to be treated gently to prevent ventricular fibrillation which could be fatal.

'I've phoned for an ambulance,' Anna told him as she knelt beside the man. She was calm now that Glenn was safe. 'There's a faint heartbeat and an even fainter pulse, but he's alive and we have to get his body heat up fast or it could be hypothermia that kills him...and you, too, if you don't get into some dry clothes quickly.'

She was getting to her feet and flinging the car door open even as she spoke. Grabbing a couple of blankets off the back seat that she used to cover the children if they fell asleep while they were driving, she eased the man up gently and with Glenn's help took off his sodden clothes and wrapped him in the blankets then held him close to transfer some body heat.

The warden had given Glenn his thick jacket, and even though he also was very cold he was in control, checking that the man was still breathing and that his tongue hadn't gone back in his mouth to choke him.

An ambulance screeched up alongside them at that moment and as paramedics spilled out with foil to wrap around them, the one in charge said to Glenn, 'You'd better come along to A and E as well. We need to keep an eye on you, too.'

'All right,' he agreed tersely, 'but I'll skip the foil. I'm not so cold that I need that. A warm bath would thaw me out. Or a brandy.'

'The bath yes,' he was told with a smile, 'but I

wouldn't advise the brandy.' Turning to Anna, he asked, 'Are you going to come along to keep an eye on him?'

Was she! At that moment the thought of letting Glenn out of her sight even for a moment was not to be considered. 'Yes,' she told him. Observing the dog that was cowering beside the stretcher that held his master, she went on, 'What about Goldie, the innocent cause of what could have been a terrible tragedy?'

'I'll see to him,' the warden said. 'There's an address on his collar. It will give me an opportunity to tell the guy's family what has happened. But I won't be away long,' he said grimly, his glance on the gaping hole in the ice. 'I'm not going to rest easy until this lot is gone.'

The staff in Accident and Emergency at St Gabriel's had been working on the man who'd nearly drowned ever since he'd been brought in. Luckily he was recovering well. At the same time Glenn was being checked over for signs of hypothermia, with Anna hovering closely beside him.

She hadn't said much. Having had a glimpse of what the world would be like without him in it she was still numb at the thought of it, and he glanced at her questioningly a few times.

So far they'd only discussed practical matters, such as letting James know what had happened and when Anna was going to pick her car up from the lakeside, which seemed of so little importance she couldn't believe they had nothing better to talk about.

As Glenn was about to leave the hospital in some dry clothes that had been found for him and having been passed as fit to go, the dog owner's wife appeared, asking if she could have a word.

'We've only just moved into Willowmere and love it here,' she told them. 'I only hope that my poor husband's awful experience won't make him disenchanted with the place. Goldie is a very naughty dog, but his master won't have a word said against him. So I'm just thankful that someone as resourceful as you was at hand, Dr Hamilton. Do, please, accept my most heartfelt thanks for what you did.'

Once she'd gone he said, 'Let's go, Anna. James has two of us missing from the practice and we can't have that. Though I think my present outfit will have to be changed before I put in an appearance.'

'How can you be so casual about something that could have cost you your life?' she asked in a voice thickening with tears.

'I wasn't exactly wrapped in cotton wool when I worked abroad, you know,' he said whimsically. 'There were a few hairy moments when I thought my time had come and there would be no one to mourn me.'

She couldn't bear the thought. How could he speak so lightly of such things when the feeling of being so alone must have been terrible? *It was not going to happen ever again. As long as she lived she would be there for him if he wanted her,* she vowed, *but she wouldn't ask for any commitment.*

Today she could have lost him and the terror of those moments at the lake would stay with her for ever. 'It was only by chance that I was there when you needed me,' she told him. 'If I hadn't been going to pick up the turkey, I would have been getting ready to go to the surgery or been already there.'

He was still in a light-hearted mood. 'So we have a

frisky dog to blame for what happened and a plump bird to thank. Maybe next time we'll manage to pick up the turkey without any diversions.'

'We?'

'Yes. We'll go together.'

It was lunchtime when they put in an appearance at the surgery. A taxi had taken them home and while Glenn had gone to shower and change his clothes Anna had gone to pick up her car.

The lake was deserted except for the warden and as the ice was melting fast he wasn't expecting to be there much longer. As she stood at the water's edge beside the graceful willows, she was filled with thankfulness that no harm had come to Glenn and in that moment everything had changed.

She knew what she had to do. It might take him away from her for ever yet he was probably going to leave anyway. But before he went he deserved to know the truth so that at last there was honesty between them. The honesty that she'd shied away from all this time. She hoped her deceit wouldn't make him think too badly of her.

# CHAPTER TEN

THE rescue at the lake was the main topic of conversation amongst staff and patients during the afternoon at the surgery. Someone had seen the ambulance driving away from the lake and approached the warden to ask him what was wrong. When he'd explained, the grapevine had swung into action.

While Glenn was answering all questions good-naturedly, Anna still had little to say, and James took her on one side and asked if she was all right. 'I know you had an awful experience this morning,' he said, 'and feel that you're in a state of shock. I can imagine what was going through your mind as you watched Glenn risking his life on the ice. Go home and rest, Anna.'

She shook her head. 'I'm fine, James. I'm just so happy to have him safe I'm lost for words. Life without him would have had no meaning.'

If she told him that what had happened by the lake had made her realise that she couldn't go on deceiving Glenn any longer, she knew that James would be supportive of her decision and would be there for her in the days ahead, but until the deed was done she felt that she couldn't talk about it to anyone.

She had to find the right moment to tell Glenn the truth and until then everything else must stay as it was.

Like James, Glenn had been watching her as the afternoon progressed. He kept remembering Anna's white face when he'd asked her if she could manage the line during those dreadful moments by the lake, and though he knew she'd been terrified on his behalf, she hadn't had much to say since.

He needed to know what she was thinking, but the opportunity to ask her didn't present itself. She went early to relieve Jess, as she'd done the day before, and he was left wondering if she was debating whether she would want to be tied to such a risk-taker should the opportunity ever arise.

Maybe they would have the chance to talk in the early evening if he suggested they go to pick up the turkey. Every moment alone with her was precious and today in particular they'd not had any time by themselves.

When Anna went upstairs to kiss the children goodnight after James had given them their bath, she held them extra close and a lump came in her throat. She swallowed hard and saw that he was watching her.

'We need to talk,' he said gravely, 'and now is a good time. Glenn has gone back to the surgery to write up some patient's notes that he didn't get the chance to do earlier.'

'I'm going to tell him the truth,' she told him flatly.

'What has made you change your mind?' he wanted to know.

'This morning at the lake. If he'd fallen through the ice, like the man with the dog did, they could have both been drowned. And when I thought of how he could have perished out there, without ever knowing why I did what I did all that time ago, I knew that I owed him the truth.'

'I guessed that something like that was going through your mind when you were so quiet this afternoon,' he told her, 'but hear me out first. I've been making some arrangements over the last couple of days and would welcome your approval.'

'What sort of arrangements?' she asked slowly in the same flat tone.

He motioned for her to go downstairs, and after tucking the children in, followed her.

'They are arrangements that will leave you free to lead your own life,' he told her gently. 'I've found a nanny for the children and a housekeeper. So you can go to the man you love with an easy mind.'

She'd lowered herself onto the nearest chair and looked at him with amazed eyes. 'You make it sound as if it was all so easy,' she breathed. 'Glenn will hate me for what I've done to him, keeping him dangling on a string when I have nothing to give him. And are you sure that the children will be happy and safe with these people that you've found? Because I don't see myself going anywhere in the near future.'

'Yes, I'm sure that the children will be happy,' he said confidently. 'I can't believe you haven't guessed who they are. Who is the one person you would trust Pollyanna and Jolyon with?'

'Jess!' she exclaimed.

'Yes. I've offered Jess what she has been looking for and she's delighted, and making an evening meal and keeping the place tidy for a few hours each day is what Helen has agreed to do. So, no matter what happens in your life, the opportunity is going to be there for you to grasp whenever you wish.'

'You are offering me peace of mind regarding the children and I love you for it, James,' she said wistfully, 'but I mean it when I say I don't expect to be going any- where. I wasn't before and I won't be now.'

At that moment Glenn returned from the surgery and asked if she wanted to make a second attempt at picking up the turkey.

'Yes, why not?' she agreed, and knew with a sinking feeling inside that yet another opportunity was being presented to her, and this one she had to take, no matter what the consequences.

'You are still looking fraught,' he commented as they drove to the farm. 'I was worried about you this after- noon. You were so quiet.'

'I was still traumatised from the morning's happen- ings,' she said. 'I thought I was going to lose you in the very place that I love so much.'

'I hope it hasn't spoilt it for you. It would be awful if it had.'

'There are worse things than that.'

'Such as?'

'I'll explain on our way back from the farm.'

'So you're going to keep me in suspense?'

It would be less hurtful than ignorance, she thought grimly, and didn't reply.

They'd collected the turkey and been offered a sherry and a mince pie, and now were on their homeward journey. As they approached the turning that led to the lake Anna said, 'Will you pull in by the lakeside, Glenn?'

'Er, yes, if you're sure,' he said doubtfully.

*'I'm sure.'*

The scene before them was as beautiful as it had ever been, with the water rippling gently beneath trees festooned with coloured lights, and Glenn said, 'It's hard to believe what it was like here this morning, isn't it?'

'Yes,' she murmured, and turned to face him. 'I have something to say to you.'

He frowned, hoping it wasn't the beginning of the long goodbye. 'What is it?' he asked abruptly.

She took a deep breath. 'I haven't been honest with you for a long time, Glenn, and now I want to put the record straight.'

'I'm listening,' he said levelly.

'Do you remember when you came to see why I hadn't joined you in Africa?'

'It is something I'm not ever likely to forget. Being told that one is no longer loved is something not easily forgotten.'

He saw her flinch and without replying Anna got out of the car and went to stand at the water's edge. He followed and as they stood side by side she said, 'There was a reason.'

'Yes. You explained at the time and I had no defence against it, not where motherless children were concerned.'

'That was partly it, but it could have been sorted by us living here in Willowmere, as you suggested, close to James and the twins, without us breaking up.'

'Exactly, but you weren't prepared to agree to that, were you?' he said, wondering where all this was leading.

'I couldn't, as it would have made no difference to the real problem.'

'And what was that?'

She took a deep breath. 'Do you remember me telling you that I'd been hurt in the car crash that killed Julie?'

'Yes, of course I do, and before I could ask how you were and show my deep concern, you gave me my marching orders in such a way that every other thought was wiped from my mind.'

'I'd only been out of hospital a few days when you showed up and was still trying to adjust to what had happened to me while I was in there,' she explained.

'I know,' he said gently. 'It must have been dreadful every time you thought about your sister-in-law and your brother left with two children to bring up on his own.'

'It was,' she agreed bleakly. 'But there was something else that had shattered all my hopes and dreams. I had severe internal injuries and was told by a gynaecologist that he had no choice but to operate. I had to have a hysterectomy and came out of hospital knowing I would never be able to give you the children that you want so much. I couldn't put you in a position where you had to choose between me and a family so I told you that it was over between us without giving you the true reason.'

As she'd been speaking Anna had watched the colour drain from his face, seen the horrified dismay in his expression, and known that she hadn't been wrong in imagining how he would react to what she'd had to tell him.

Maybe it had been a mistake and she should have carried on with the miserable charade, but at least she'd given Glenn the chance to walk away from her child-lessness now that he knew the truth.

His face was a frozen mask of pain as he asked, 'How could you keep that from me?'

Feeling as if her heart would break, she cringed away from him.

'I can't believe that you have placed such a dreadful burden upon yourself and have carried it alone for all this time,' he continued, and she became still. 'Yes, I want children, Anna, but I want you even more. How could you ever think otherwise? And if we did want children, there are so many desperately needing loving parents. Our home need never be empty of them.' He was smiling now and gently stroked her cheek. 'Even though I wish you'd told me before, I'm humbled to know how much you must have loved me at that time to send me away like you did.'

As his words filtered through, Anna's heart swelled with hope and happiness. 'Nothing has changed,' she said softly. 'I've never stopped loving you and I never will. I honestly thought it was the right thing to do, and I'm so sorry for all the wasted years...'

He pulled her into his arms, stopping her stumbling words with kisses, and Anna knew that she was finally where she belonged. Not hopefully but *completely*.

'We've got the rest of our lives to make up for lost time,' he said, his lips now against her brow. 'What I want to know is, will you marry me, Anna?'

She was weeping, sparkling drops on her lashes like diamonds as she sobbed, 'Yes, I will marry you, Glenn. I do love you so much.'

'And I love you too, more than anything or anyone else on earth,' he told her softly.

She looked at him, her eyes luminous with the tears. 'So you're not asking me out of pity?'

'Pity!' he exclaimed. 'Pity! Of course not. I came to Willowmere to see if there was any hope of us getting back together before I accepted what I thought was the inevitable, and there have been times when I've felt that the magic was still there, but you wouldn't admit it.'

'I was afraid to. You're a kind and decent man and I couldn't bear the thought of you taking me on out of compassion if I told you about my childlessness, but after this morning, when I thought I might lose you for ever, I knew I couldn't let you go on thinking that I didn't love you.'

As his arms tightened around her he said whimsically, 'It was worth crawling over the freezing ice and having to fish that poor fellow out of the water with it crumbling all around us just to hear you say that you'll marry me. What about the children, though? I can't carry you off to Africa while they need you.'

'James has sorted it. He'd guessed how we feel about each other and has found himself a great nanny in Jess, and Helen, who was our housekeeper when he and I were young, has agreed to cook the meals and keep the house clean.'

'So the way ahead is clear,' he said jubilantly. 'I can't believe it! If we go to Africa, it need only be for a year or so, then you won't be away from the children too long, or we can stay here in Willowmere if you'd rather not.'

She shook her head. 'No. I was just as keen as you to go there in the old days and nothing has changed, so let's go and tell James our wonderful news.'

'Yes, let's,' he said triumphantly, and kissed her thoroughly again before they went back to the car and drove back to Bracken House.

James had been delighted to hear what they'd had to say when they'd returned with the turkey and had suggested, 'How about we invite a few friends round for a drink tomorrow night to tell them your glad tidings? I can't think of a better time to celebrate than Christmas Eve.'

They'd agreed and then gone next door to the annexe, and once inside Glenn had produced a beautiful emerald ring that had been his grandmother's. 'She was the only other woman I've ever loved,' he said gravely, 'and ever since I've come to Willowmere I've carried it with me. Green and gold are your colours, aren't they, Anna? But if you don't like it, we can choose something else.'

'It's beautiful,' she said. 'I can tell that it means a lot to you and I'd love to wear it.' She held out her hand and he slipped the ring slowly on to her finger. As they both looked down at it the future that they'd never expected to be theirs was opening up in front of them.

When the children were told the next morning that there was to be a wedding, the thrill for Polly of discovering that she was to be a bridesmaid in a pretty dress almost equalled the excitement of Christmas. Jolyon greeted the news of his future role of pageboy with his usual reserve, but seemed to approve.

As Anna and Glenn had sat talking late into the night they'd decided to arrange the wedding for the end of January. Until that time everything would stay as it was at the surgery, and in their domestic situations he was going to move in with her. At Bracken House Jess and Helen would step into their roles in the lives of James and the children, and by the time she was ready to leave for foreign lands with Glenn, Pollyanna and Jolyon would be used to the new arrangements.

At the party that night were Jess and her parents, Georgina and the blond man she'd danced with at the ball, who she introduced as Nicholas, Elaine, and Clare and her mother, and when James announced the reason for the gathering, there was much surprise and excitement.

'We're not going to lose you both, are we?' Georgina asked them.

Anna replied, 'Yes, but not for too long. We'll be coming back to Willowmere to live. The wedding is at the end of January and then we're flying out to Africa.'

'Yes,' Glenn agreed. 'We'll be back again in time for next Christmas. That will be long enough away for both of us.'

The guests had left, James had gone up to bed, and as the fingers of the clock moved to twelve, Glenn took Anna in his arms and said softly, 'At one time I thought that the only way I would ever get to hold you like this would be under the mistletoe. I never dreamt that here was where you'd want to be.'

His glance went to the children's presents, ready and waiting under the tree, alongside the traditional sherry and mince pie that had been left out for Santa, and he smiled.

'James usually polishes those off,' she told him. 'He must have forgotten in all the excitement, so you had better do the honours. It wouldn't do for the children to find that Santa hadn't had his snack when they get up.'

'No sooner said than done,' he agreed, 'and then I have a present for you.'

When he gave her the watercolour she was entranced. 'It's beautiful,' she told him, 'and is going to go with me wherever I go.'

'Even though your love of the place was almost destroyed by what occurred when the ice broke?' he questioned. 'I'd almost decided not to give you the picture after that, but you brought the magic back to Willow Lake by what you did in the evening.'

With his voice deepening, he went on, 'I won't ever forget that moment. You brought me out of darkness into light when you told me that you still loved me. Suddenly I could see the way ahead.'

As daylight began to creep over Willowmere on Christmas morning, the church bells rang out into the silence that hung over the village, and as the two men watched the children's delight in all the things that Santa had brought, Anna said, 'I'm going to take some flowers to Clare. I won't be long.'

She lived in the apartment above the gallery and when Anna rang the doorbell Clare appeared with a robe over her nightdress and exclaimed, 'Anna! Merry Christmas!'

'I've brought these for you,' she told her, handing her an arrangement of red roses. 'They are just to say that I'm thinking of you, and to ask if you and your mum would like to come round for coffee when some of the excitement that Santa's visit generates has calmed down a little.'

'That would be lovely,' Clare said, and almost as if she'd read Anna's mind, she added, 'I've got my appointment to have a consultation with an oncologist between Christmas and New Year, so that's good, isn't it?'

'Yes, it is,' she agreed, and as she wished her goodbye she hoped that the news that Clare was dreading might not be quite as devastating as she was expecting it to be.

It was raining, a sudden shower, and she had no umbrella, but there was something else she had to do now that the flowers had been delivered. Something that she wanted to do on her own while the only people about were herself and the bellringers.

Julie's grave was in a quiet corner of the churchyard. At this time of year there were snowdrops on it, tiny white flowers with drooping heads. Later in the day James would come with sweet-scented lilies for *his* moment of remembrance, but now it was just her, wanting to know if she had the blessing of the children's mother and hoping that she might feel Julie's presence near her in the churchyard.

The rain had stopped as suddenly as it had started, and a watery sun was shining up above as she stood beside the grave in silence, but the feeling that Julie was close by wasn't there.

What had she expected? she asked herself. Those other times when she'd felt Julie had been near could have been imagination, tricks of the mind or wishful thinking. The minutes were ticking by and, cold and wet, she turned to go despondently.

It was then that she saw it, arched in the sky, beautiful beyond compare, a rainbow, and if there was one thing that Julie had loved to see, it had been a rainbow.

On the day that she, Anna, had been discharged from hospital, James had brought the babies with him when he'd gone to fetch her, and as they'd driven home with her on the back seat beside the two baby carriers, she'd been in the depths of grief and despair until she'd looked out of the car window and seen a rainbow in the sky.

There had been one after the other all the way home and for the first time in days she'd found a degree of comfort because it had seemed as if Julie was somewhere near and from that feeling had come the strength to face what lay ahead.

When she reached the lychgate at the entrance to the churchyard Glenn was standing there and she asked, 'How long have you been here?'

He put his arms around her and held her close. 'Long enough to know that there was one thing you still had to do before you could move on. Did you get the answer you wanted?'

The rainbow was fading slowly but she was smiling as she looked up at her future husband. 'Yes, my love. I did.'

## SEPTEMBER 2008 HARDBACK TITLES

# ROMANCE

| | |
|---|---|
| **Ruthlessly Bedded by the Italian Billionaire** *Emma Darcy* | 978 0 263 20350 9 |
| **Mendez's Mistress** *Anne Mather* | 978 0 263 20351 6 |
| **Rafael's Suitable Bride** *Cathy Williams* | 978 0 263 20352 3 |
| **Desert Prince, Defiant Virgin** *Kim Lawrence* | 978 0 263 20353 0 |
| **Sicilian Husband, Unexpected Baby** *Sharon Kendrick* | 978 0 263 20354 7 |
| **Hired: The Italian's Convenient Mistress** *Carol Marinelli* | 978 0 263 20355 4 |
| **Antonides' Forbidden Wife** *Anne McAllister* | 978 0 263 20356 1 |
| **The Millionaire's Chosen Bride** *Susanne James* | 978 0 263 20357 8 |
| **Wedded in a Whirlwind** *Liz Fielding* | 978 0 263 20358 5 |
| **Blind Date with the Boss** *Barbara Hannay* | 978 0 263 20359 2 |
| **The Tycoon's Christmas Proposal** *Jackie Braun* | 978 0 263 20360 8 |
| **Christmas Wishes, Mistletoe Kisses** *Fiona Harper* | 978 0 263 20361 5 |
| **Rescued by the Magic of Christmas** *Melissa McClone* | 978 0 263 20362 2 |
| **Her Millionaire, His Miracle** *Myrna Mackenzie* | 978 0 263 20363 9 |
| **Italian Doctor, Sleigh-Bell Bride** *Sarah Morgan* | 978 0 263 20364 6 |
| **The Desert Surgeon's Secret Son** *Olivia Gates* | 978 0 263 20365 3 |

# HISTORICAL

| | |
|---|---|
| **Scandalous Secret, Defiant Bride** *Helen Dickson* | 978 0 263 20210 6 |
| **A Question of Impropriety** *Michelle Styles* | 978 0 263 20211 3 |
| **Conquering Knight, Captive Lady** *Anne O'Brien* | 978 0 263 20212 0 |

# MEDICAL™

| | |
|---|---|
| **Dr Devereux's Proposal** *Margaret McDonagh* | 978 0 263 19910 9 |
| **Children's Doctor, Meant-to-be Wife** *Meredith Webber* | 978 0 263 19911 6 |
| **Christmas at Willowmere** *Abigail Gordon* | 978 0 263 19912 3 |
| **Dr Romano's Christmas Baby** *Amy Andrews* | 978 0 263 19913 0 |

# MILLS & BOON®
*Pure reading pleasure*™

# SEPTEMBER 2008 LARGE PRINT TITLES

## ROMANCE

| | |
|---|---|
| The Markonos Bride *Michelle Reid* | 978 0 263 20074 4 |
| The Italian's Passionate Revenge *Lucy Gordon* | 978 0 263 20075 1 |
| The Greek Tycoon's Baby Bargain *Sharon Kendrick* | 978 0 263 20076 8 |
| Di Cesare's Pregnant Mistress *Chantelle Shaw* | 978 0 263 20077 5 |
| His Pregnant Housekeeper *Caroline Anderson* | 978 0 263 20078 2 |
| The Italian Playboy's Secret Son *Rebecca Winters* | 978 0 263 20079 9 |
| Her Sheikh Boss *Carol Grace* | 978 0 263 20080 5 |
| Wanted: White Wedding *Natasha Oakley* | 978 0 263 20081 2 |

## HISTORICAL

| | |
|---|---|
| The Last Rake In London *Nicola Cornick* | 978 0 263 20166 6 |
| The Outrageous Lady Felsham *Louise Allen* | 978 0 263 20167 3 |
| An Unconventional Miss *Dorothy Elbury* | 978 0 263 20168 0 |

## MEDICAL™

| | |
|---|---|
| The Surgeon's Fatherhood Surprise *Jennifer Taylor* | 978 0 263 19974 1 |
| The Italian Surgeon Claims His Bride *Alison Roberts* | 978 0 263 19975 8 |
| Desert Doctor, Secret Sheikh *Meredith Webber* | 978 0 263 19976 5 |
| A Wedding in Warragurra *Fiona Lowe* | 978 0 263 19977 2 |
| The Firefighter and the Single Mum *Laura Iding* | 978 0 263 19978 9 |
| The Nurse's Little Miracle *Molly Evans* | 978 0 263 19979 6 |

## MILLS & BOON®
*Pure reading pleasure*™

# OCTOBER 2008 HARDBACK TITLES

## ROMANCE

| | |
|---|---|
| **The Greek Tycoon's Disobedient Bride** *Lynne Graham* | 978 0 263 20366 0 |
| **The Venetian's Midnight Mistress** *Carole Mortimer* | 978 0 263 20367 7 |
| **Ruthless Tycoon, Innocent Wife** *Helen Brooks* | 978 0 263 20368 4 |
| **The Sheikh's Wayward Wife** *Sandra Marton* | 978 0 263 20369 1 |
| **The Fiorenza Forced Marriage** *Melanie Milburne* | 978 0 263 20370 7 |
| **The Spanish Billionaire's Christmas Bride** *Maggie Cox* | 978 0 263 20371 4 |
| **The Ruthless Italian's Inexperienced Wife** *Christina Hollis* | 978 0 263 20372 1 |
| **Claimed for the Italian's Revenge** *Natalie Rivers* | 978 0 263 20373 8 |
| **The Italian's Christmas Miracle** *Lucy Gordon* | 978 0 263 20374 5 |
| **Cinderella and the Cowboy** *Judy Christenberry* | 978 0 263 20375 2 |
| **His Mistletoe Bride** *Cara Colter* | 978 0 263 20376 9 |
| **Pregnant: Father Wanted** *Claire Baxter* | 978 0 263 20377 6 |
| **Marry-Me Christmas** *Shirley Jump* | 978 0 263 20378 3 |
| **Her Baby's First Christmas** *Susan Meier* | 978 0 263 20379 0 |
| **One Magical Christmas** *Carol Marinelli* | 978 0 263 20380 6 |
| **The GP's Meant-To-Be Bride** *Jennifer Taylor* | 978 0 263 20381 3 |

## HISTORICAL

| | |
|---|---|
| **Miss Winbolt and the Fortune Hunter** *Sylvia Andrew* | 978 0 263 20213 7 |
| **Captain Fawley's Innocent Bride** *Annie Burrows* | 978 0 263 20214 4 |
| **The Rake's Rebellious Lady** *Anne Herries* | 978 0 263 20215 1 |

## MEDICAL™

| | |
|---|---|
| **A Mummy for Christmas** *Caroline Anderson* | 978 0 263 19914 7 |
| **A Bride and Child Worth Waiting For** *Marion Lennox* | 978 0 263 19915 4 |
| **The Italian Surgeon's Christmas Miracle** *Alison Roberts* | 978 0 263 19916 1 |
| **Children's Doctor, Christmas Bride** *Lucy Clark* | 978 0 263 19917 8 |

## MILLS & BOON®
*Pure reading pleasure™*

# OCTOBER 2008 LARGE PRINT TITLES

## ROMANCE

| | |
|---|---|
| **The Sheikh's Blackmailed Mistress** *Penny Jordan* | 978 0 263 20082 9 |
| **The Millionaire's Inexperienced Love-Slave** *Miranda Lee* | 978 0 263 20083 6 |
| **Bought: The Greek's Innocent Virgin** *Sarah Morgan* | 978 0 263 20084 3 |
| **Bedded at the Billionaire's Convenience** *Cathy Williams* | 978 0 263 20085 0 |
| **The Pregnancy Promise** *Barbara McMahon* | 978 0 263 20086 7 |
| **The Italian's Cinderella Bride** *Lucy Gordon* | 978 0 263 20087 4 |
| **Saying Yes to the Millionaire** *Fiona Harper* | 978 0 263 20088 1 |
| **Her Royal Wedding Wish** *Cara Colter* | 978 0 263 20089 8 |

## HISTORICAL

| | |
|---|---|
| **Untouched Mistress** *Margaret McPhee* | 978 0 263 20169 7 |
| **A Less Than Perfect Lady** *Elizabeth Beacon* | 978 0 263 20170 3 |
| **Viking Warrior, Unwilling Wife** *Michelle Styles* | 978 0 263 20171 0 |

## MEDICAL™

| | |
|---|---|
| **The Doctor's Royal Love-Child** *Kate Hardy* | 978 0 263 19980 2 |
| **His Island Bride** *Marion Lennox* | 978 0 263 19981 9 |
| **A Consultant Beyond Compare** *Joanna Neil* | 978 0 263 19982 6 |
| **The Surgeon Boss's Bride** *Melanie Milburne* | 978 0 263 19983 3 |
| **A Wife Worth Waiting For** *Maggie Kingsley* | 978 0 263 19984 0 |
| **Desert Prince, Expectant Mother** *Olivia Gates* | 978 0 263 19985 7 |